Follow the
Leader

Follow the Leader

BY VICKI WINSLOW

ILLUSTRATED BY COLIN BOOTMAN

DELACORTE PRESS

Sincere thanks to Wendy Lamb,
a truly inspiring editor

Published by
Delacorte Press
Bantam Doubleday Dell Publishing Group, Inc.
1540 Broadway
New York, New York 10036

Library of Congress Cataloging-in-Publication Data

Winslow, Vicki.
    Follow the Leader / Vicki Winslow.
        p.   cm.
    Summary: In 1971 in a small North Carolina town, eleven-year-old Amanda
must deal with being bused to a newly integrated, formerly all-black school
and being separated from her best friend, who has chosen a private school.
    ISBN 0-385-32285-2
    [1. Race relations—Fiction.   2. Schools—Fiction.   3. Prejudices—Fiction.
4. Afro-Americans—Fiction.   5. Friendship—Fiction.   6. North Carolina—
Fiction.]   I. Title.
PZ7.W7518Ge   1997
[Fic]—dc21
                                                    97-4991
                                                    CIP
                                                    AC

The text of this book is set in 12–point Garamond 3.
Book design by Kimberly M. Adlerman

*This book is dedicated to
my grandmother, Mary Pleasant Winslow;
to my parents,
Robert Morris Winslow and
Virginia Forehand Winslow;
and to Tom—with all my heart.*

CHAPTER 1

"Mom!" I yelled. Then Jackie and I both lay real still in the twin beds in my room and waited.

Mom didn't actually come into the room—she just cracked the door. Her eyebrow was pointing up in the middle, so I could tell I was annoying her. "What is it, Amanda?" she asked.

"Mom, will you please measure our hair?"

The eyebrow went back down, and I saw one-half of a pretty good smile. "I'll be right back," Mom said.

It was the summer of 1971. I was in between fifth grade and sixth grade. My best friend, Jackie Charles, and I were both eleven years old and having the time of our lives. Summer vacation was magic: school was out, swimming and running around barefoot were allowed, and the major food groups were hamburgers, hot dogs, watermelon, and homemade ice cream. It stayed light until after nine o'clock, and even then there were lightning bugs to chase and no reason to go to bed early.

Mom came back, unrolling her tape measure. "All right, girls," she said, "you know the drill." Mom had been measuring our hair ever since second grade, when Jackie and I got into a fight about whose hair was longer. Mom had pulled out her tape measure to make us both shut up, and after that we had two new traditions. One was that we kept measuring our hair to see how long it was getting, and the other was that anytime Jackie and I started to fuss and my Mom heard us, she'd bring in the tape measure. Usually just seeing it was enough to make us both start laughing and forget what we were fighting about.

Jackie and I wore our hair the same way—almost to our shoulders, with bangs that we sometimes pushed back with a headband. The only difference was that Jackie's hair was dark brown, and mine was light brown. We spread our hair out as far as it would go, and Mom put one end of the tape measure on our scalps and the other at the longest piece of hair on the pillow. She did Jackie first, then me. I loved feeling the tape measure in my hair. It made me feel like Rapunzel, like I had yards and yards of golden hair cascading down my back in natural curls. I really had plain straight hair that never seemed to grow past my shoulders, no matter what.

"Your bangs need to be cut," Mom said as she measured my hair. "From scalp to tip-end, you're measuring eight and one-eighth inches today," she said. "Jackie, it looks like you win today, with a length of eight and five-eighths. Congratulations. Now don't you think it's time you both got out of bed and ate some lunch?"

Lunch was my favorite food—Chef Boyardee pizza from a box. Mom always added mozzarella cheese to the parmesan that came in the kit, but there was no drowning out that parmesan smell as it baked.

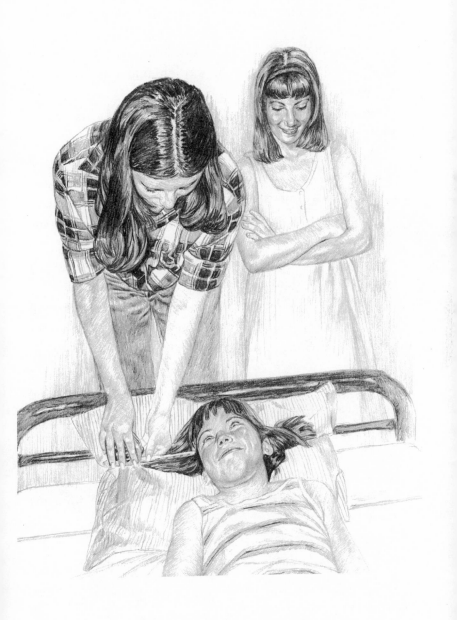

"It's like dirty feet!" Jackie said, and it really was. "It's feetsa!"

"Pepperoni feetsa," I said.

"You're spoiling my lunch for me, here," Dad said. He had come home for lunch since he was building a house not too far away. After we ate, he challenged Jackie and me to a quick game of one-on-two at the basketball goal in our backyard.

Dad was a basketball freak. He taught me how to play when I was about six years old. I had developed into an excellent free-throw shooter, and I had a mean layup. Dad claimed it wasn't very effective, because once I'd done it any decent player could see it coming and block it. But he told me I jumped so well that if I were only three feet taller, I could probably dunk the ball.

So anyway, Dad had just scored, and he threw me the ball so I could take it back. "There's an outdoor concert at the school this evening," he said. "I think it would be fun for us to go."

Jackie twisted her mouth up and pulled her headband down over her forehead. Then she snapped it back in place, but it was in the wrong spot. It made her bangs stick up like spikes.

"You have no soul," I told her. "I *love* music." I put my left hand over my heart, and Dad stole the ball from my right hand.

"Oh, I'll go with you," Jackie said. "I got nothing better to do. I'll call Mama and tell her I'm spending the night again."

Jackie spent the night with me so much that she kept a nightgown and toothbrush at my house. We went to the same church and the same school, and, as I mentioned, we wore our hair the same way. One year we went to our church Halloween party dressed as Siamese twins. We had found this really big poncho at the PTA Thrift Store, and my mom had widened the hole so that we could both get our heads through. Then we just wore our regular clothes underneath, but it did look like we were joined at the shoulders. After that, a lot of the other kids at church called us the Siamese Twins.

But the truth was, inside we were completely different. I loved music, and I had played the piano since I was pretty young. I liked to read and daydream and imagine what it would be like to be somebody else, somebody in another country. I liked to imagine so much, I think, because inside I was afraid of so many things—getting hurt, making people mad, doing the wrong thing.

Jackie Charles wasn't afraid of anything. She was the funniest person you could ever meet, and she loved excitement. She would make me ride with her in the first car of the fastest roller-coaster at Frontier Village Theme Park, and she used to spend the whole three and a half minutes yelling, "Keep your arms up! Keep your arms up!" She kept hers up even during the sudden, steep turn that plunged you down into the tunnel, when it looked like your arms (and maybe even your head) would surely get knocked off.

We were watching TV at my house when Neil Armstrong walked on the moon, and Jackie said, "I'm going to be an astronaut. *I* want to walk on the moon!" She didn't change her mind when *Apollo 13* almost didn't make it back to Earth. "It's an adventure," she said. "Like Columbus discovering America!"

I didn't like adventure, and if it had been up to me America would have stayed undiscovered, so I don't know why Jackie liked me. Sometimes I wondered if it was just because I was *convenient*. Or maybe it was because I would usually go along with her plans. It didn't really matter to me *why* Jackie was my friend. I just felt lucky to have her.

CHAPTER 2

On the way to the concert, we dropped Laura off at Barney's, the ice cream place near the highway where she worked for the summer. She got to wear a little uniform with cute buttons shaped like ice cream cones. Laura said they might be cute, but it was a pain in the *derrière* pushing them through the buttonholes. Laura has taken three years of French, which is why she called her rear end her *derrière*.

"I'll get a ride home with Angie," she said as she jumped out of the car. "Bye."

"I wish I was old enough to work at Barney's," Jackie said. All the teenagers in the universe seemed to live there during the summer.

"Yeah," I said, "but Laura says it's really sticky and her hair always smells like maraschino cherries."

"Nothing in life is ever perfect," Dad said.

When we got to the school, Mom spread some blankets on the grass.

Mom had brought my bee-sting blanket—I call it that because it was the same blanket Dad wrapped me in the night I had to go to the emergency room with an allergic reaction to a bee sting. That happened when I was four years old. The bee-sting blanket was actually a comforter made out of flowered nylon with a layer of fluffy stuff in the middle that was beginning to leak out a little. When I was little I called it my bumbie.

Jackie and I sat on the bee-sting blanket and waited for the music to start.

"Rock and roll!" Jackie said, snapping her fingers and swaying from side to side on her knees.

"Actually, it's classical," Dad said. "I hope that isn't a problem."

"Nah," Jackie said, jamming her headband in place. "Just wake me up when it's over."

Jackie fell asleep in the middle of the very first song, "Jesu, Joy of Man's Desiring." It was a beautiful, quiet song, and it's even more beautiful when you're outside sitting on your favorite fluffy comforter. I felt the same way I feel when I'm at my grandma Braverman's house—like there's too much to eat, and I want to eat it *all.* To make it even better, past the edge of the softball field I had a view of a mountain range called the Seven Sisters. The mountains were way off in the distance, so they looked like one of the blue chalk lines that Dad snaps against a piece of Sheetrock when he's building houses and needs to mark a straight line. They seemed cold and mysterious.

After the first song was finished and the audience had stopped clapping, the silence seemed to go on too long. I watched the conductor to see what was going to happen next. Had he forgotten what he was doing? No, apparently he was just building up suspense before he played the most fantastic song in the world. He raised his stick, pointed it straight out, then brought it down. It seemed almost like a magic wand, drawing music out of the sky and the faraway mountains. At first, just one instrument began to play—a clarinet, or maybe a bassoon. It sounded simple, lonesome and clear, and then a second one joined the first, and then the whole orchestra joined in, and the more the instruments played, the harder the conductor waved his baton.

I have never heard anything so beautiful, or seen anything so impossible. I wanted to stand up, and cry, and go crazy all at one time. You can't feel like that for very long, or you probably *would* go crazy.

I clapped so hard after that song that Jackie even opened her eyes and stared at me for a second before she closed them again.

"Mom!" I said. "What was the name of that song?"

"That was Bach again," Mom said, reading from her program. "It was called Fugue in G Minor (the 'Little')."

The "Little Fugue." I wanted to say the Pledge of Allegiance right then and there, or say something quiet and solemn like wedding vows or the words on a tombstone. I know it sounds stupid. But that's the way I felt.

I didn't hear anything else that the orchestra played. I just lay there beside Jackie on the bee-sting blanket and looked up into the sky and heard that song playing over and over. And while the music played in my head, I kept seeing pictures of the best place in the whole world: Sapphire Mountain.

Sapphire Mountain was the prettiest of the Seven Sisters. We rented a cabin up there one year for summer vacation. To get to it, you had to drive up a winding dirt road, and sometimes it was scary on one side of the car, and then suddenly it was scary on the other side. But even if you didn't feel safe, you couldn't help but look down and see all the flowers blooming. Flame azalea and rhododendron grew up there, and mountain laurel lathered the sides of the mountain like foamy soapsuds. It all smelled as good as it looked.

My sister, Laura, and I slept in the loft of the cabin, and from the window you could see a huge view. It made my eyes feel cool to look at it.

Of course, maybe that was because Sapphire Mountain was cool a lot of the time, even in summer. The air felt warm, but as you walked along you'd hit a spot of cool air. It felt like swimming in a lake, where you hit warm spots and cool spots in the water. The nights were almost always chilly, and lots of times Dad would build a fire and everybody would sit around and roast marshmallows or just sit and watch the sparks rise up in the dark. Sometimes we sang songs.

I thought about that as I lay on the blanket at the concert, and after about an hour Mom and Dad decided to go. I carried their blanket to the car while Dad carried Jackie, who never did wake up, all wrapped up in my comforter. She slept on the backseat while we drove home, and I sat beside her and tried to make the same motions the conductor had made, as if I could call the music up out of the sky myself. I saw Mom grin at Dad in the rearview mirror and knew I was being spied on. I sat on my hands the rest of the way, but inside me, the music rose up like campfire sparks.

If I were a real conductor, maybe I could have changed what happened next. But I'm not. I was caught completely by surprise, like a deer frozen in the middle of the road by the headlights of a speeding car.

CHAPTER 3

When we got up the next morning, Jackie and I played our piano duet. It wasn't anything special, because the only thing I'd ever been able to teach Jackie how to play was "Heart and Soul." She picked out the high part with one finger while I played the complicated part. We had gotten good at it—Jackie could do her part without messing up, and I could really go to town on my fancy part.

We ate blueberry muffins for breakfast, and afterward went into the living room. We sat on the floor next to the record player, talking and listening to the Beatles. We played "Let It Be" over and over, until we'd get sick of it and turn the record over to play the other side. The other side was "The Long and Winding Road." Usually hearing it once was enough to make "Let It Be" sound really good again.

"What do you want to do?" I asked her.

Jackie stood up and threw her head back. " 'Let it be, let it be,' " she sang, at the top of her lungs. " 'Let it be, aww let it be . . .' "

"We could play Secret Garden, if you want," I said.

Secret Garden was a game that I had made up based on the book. There wasn't much to it. Basically we just went down

12

to the side of my house that faced the woods and pretended that the woods were a wall that enclosed an old, neglected garden that we had discovered and were bringing back to life. The "garden" was the flowers that grew against the house on that side, and we would move the dirt around under the hydrangea bushes and marigolds with a little spade and trowel and water the roots. Sometimes we'd set up a decorative rock border around the flowers, and we would pick out some of the biggest chunks of firewood on Dad's pile and make garden benches out of them. It was fun to pretend that we were invisible behind the wall, and that we were magically helping the flowers bloom. If the firewood wasn't too full of bugs, we'd sit on the chunks and talk while we looked at the flowers. I still liked it, but Jackie wrinkled up her nose at me.

"We're getting too old to play pretend games," Jackie said. She sang the chorus of "Let It Be" again, until my mom told us to keep it down or go outside.

"We'll keep it down," Jackie promised, just to get my mom to leave the room. Jackie rolled her eyes at me. "Your mom is tough," she said. "She's as bad as Fierce Pierce."

Mrs. Pierce had been our fifth-grade teacher. Jackie gave her the name "Fierce Pierce" after the first two days of school. Mrs. Pierce was sarcastic and strict and she wore her hair in a tall sort of bubble with short bangs.

"Remember that report you wrote?" I asked her. "When you used the dictionary?" Jackie and I rolled over on the floor, laughing.

Fierce Pierce had told us to write a 200-word report about

any book we had read during the school year. Jackie had decided that the best way to get 200 words fast was to go to the dictionary and list the first 200 words. She had gotten in front of the whole class and said, "The book I read this year was the dictionary." Then she just started saying words, starting with *aardvark,* and she threw in punctuation so that it almost sounded like she was reading a poem. The last thing she said before Fierce Pierce made her sit down was, *"Abash, abate."*

"She gave me a D!" Jackie said. She was still mad about that. She thought she was so creative and different that she should get an A+.

"I wonder if Fierce Pierce will be at the new school?" I said. Our school system was being desegregated in the fall, and we'd be going to a school downtown. "When you get back from vacation, it'll only be three weeks to orientation."

My cat, Ted, walked in. I picked him up. "What are you going to wear to orientation?" I asked. I rubbed my chin against the top of Ted's gray-striped head. Ted would only put up with that sort of thing for about two minutes.

"Oh, I'm not going," Jackie said airily. She turned the record over and started playing "The Long and Winding Road."

I let Ted jump down. He barely touched the ground before he leaped onto the piano bench.

"You're not?" I asked.

"No." Jackie flipped her bangs out of her eyes and looked at me. "I'm going to private school," she said.

CHAPTER 4

"Are you serious?" I asked.

"Yeah. Mama and Daddy don't want me riding the bus for two hours every day." She flipped her bangs out of her eyes again. She didn't even act like she cared!

I had left the piano keyboard cover up, and when Ted decided to jump from the piano bench to the keyboard, it sounded exactly like I felt inside—all jangly and mixed up. Ted plunged across the keys, trying to get away from the noise. I grabbed him off the piano.

"It's no big deal," Jackie said. "Just make your folks send you to the private school, too."

I didn't think it would be that easy. My mom and dad weren't like Jackie's parents. Sometimes it seemed to me like all adults were cardboard people, or mannequins. They just cooked and worked and took care of things while all the real living was done in the real world—mine. The World of Sixth Grade, or whatever. But sometimes I did get the idea that my parents were real, too. Such as when my mom laughed hysterically at Rowan and Martin on TV, or when she got all heated up about something she thought was important, like equal pay for women or integration.

But Jackie's parents *always* seemed like cardboard. Jackie could pick them up and put them down where she wanted, like big game pieces. If she got in trouble at school, she could talk them into going to the principal to get her out of it. If a bunch of us wanted to go skating or go see a movie on Saturday when our parents were doing yard work or were busy with other things, she could always get her mom or dad to drop everything and drive us. She could never understand that I couldn't do the same thing with my parents.

Mom stuck her head in the doorway. "Jackie, your mom's here," she said. "I'm telling her you need an inch or two trimmed off your hair."

"My hair's never going to be cut again!" Jackie yelled. "Abash, abate!" she said as she turned to wave good-bye.

I just stood there, holding Ted under my chin, while Jackie flipped out the door like nothing had happened.

I stood in the middle of the kitchen. Ted's tail was whipping across my stomach. But I wasn't ready to let him go.

"I can't believe what I just heard," I said.

Mom finished wiping the kitchen counter and tossed her green sponge in the sink. "I heard, too," she said. "I guess I'm as surprised as you are."

We both stood there a minute thinking about it. "What am I going to do?" I asked.

Mom opened her mouth to say something, but the phone rang. She rolled her eyes and answered it, so I put Ted down and went to Laura's room.

Laura had her own bedroom at the opposite end of the

house from everybody else's. Her room even had its own outside door, but Dad told her not to let that give her any ideas. She had her own bathroom, too, so I didn't see all that much of her. She had turned seventeen in May and was almost a senior in high school. I could talk to Laura, though. She wasn't a snot like a lot of my friends' older brothers and sisters.

Laura opened the door, and as usual she looked great. She had long, straight brown hair, parted down the middle, and blue eyes. We look a lot alike, but it looks much better on her. Mom says I'll be fine, but I wonder. I have a thin face and huge front teeth. I'm sort of bony all over, and I don't think I'll ever need even a training bra. I brush my hair a lot to try to get it to grow faster, because I want mine to be longer than Jackie's. Dad says I've grown a real nice head of hair for somebody who was bald as a cue ball for the first three years of life.

It was almost two o'clock, but Laura had just gotten up. As she let me in she was tying the belt of her robe. "What's up, Little Bit?" she yawned.

Laura's room was bright and sunny because it had two windows and a shaggy yellow rug on the hardwood floor. She had a double brass bed, a dresser that used to belong to our grandfather, and a desk and chair. I sat down at the desk. Laura had these neat yellow glass flowers on long wire stems stuck in a 7-Up bottle as a decoration, and I wanted them for my own room. I kept thinking that if I admired them enough, she'd tell me I could have them. But right then I had more serious matters to discuss.

"Jackie's not going to be integrated," I said. "Her parents are making her go to a private school. I don't know *what* I'm going to do. What's this?" I held up a little brass thing with holes in it. "Does it have to do with drugs?" I was shocked, but I tried to sound like it was okay.

"*No,* it's not for drugs," Laura said. She laughed. "It's an incense burner, idjit."

"Oh, yeah. So anyway, what do you think about that? Do you think Mom and Dad will let me go to the private school with Jackie?"

Laura went over and pulled down one of the window shades. The shade had orange and yellow flower decals on it and a bumper sticker that said "Make Love Not War."

"No," she said. "You know Mom's really into this desegregation thing. And you know what else? So am I."

Laura sat down on the edge of her bed and looked at me. "Desegregation is something important—more important than best friends, even. You and me, Little Bit. We'll go into this thing together, like pioneers, you know? Just like the crazy pilgrims, setting sail for the New World. You have to see this thing from the right perspective, is all. It's a new world all over again."

I sighed. Every year Laura sounded more like Mom, only with a younger style. "I'm not the pioneer *type,*" I said. "I'm like the people who stayed in the Old Country and kept things going there."

"Well, in this particular case, Little Bit, the Old Country is dead. But that's a good thing, see. You don't want to live in a world where people are treated differently because of the color of their skin, do you? Think about it. What if you were the one with the 'wrong' color skin? It's like Germany, and Hitler. If you sit by and watch while people are persecuted, the next thing you know—bam! *You're* the one being persecuted. It can happen. Anyway, talk to Mom and Dad about it and hear what they have to say. They're better at making speeches than me."

Laura yawned again. She sleeps *all the time.* Mom says it's because she's a teenager.

"Okay," I said. "Thanks." I stood up.

"Don't walk off with my incense burner, either," Laura said.

"Oh, I forgot," I said. I put it back on her desk and walked out in what I hoped was a dignified way.

CHAPTER 5

———

I didn't much want to discuss desegregation with Mom and Dad. They had already explained how it was going to work: first- through fourth-graders were all going to my old school, West Windsor Elementary, and to the other elementary school in our district, Southwest Elementary. Fifth- and sixth-graders were going downtown to East Windsor Elementary. Seventh- and eighth-graders: West Windsor Junior High. Ninth- and tenth-graders: downtown to East Windsor High School. Eleventh- and twelfth-graders: West Windsor Senior High. It was complicated, but I had figured it was just something I had to put up with. It hadn't dawned on me that not everybody would go along with the plan.

Mom was in the laundry area. I said, "I'm depressed," in a real sad voice.

Both of Mom's eyebrows went up.

"I'm not going to know *anybody* at that new school. All my friends are going to private school." What I really meant was that *Jackie* was going to private school. It wouldn't have mattered to me if nobody else from our class had gone to the new school, as long as Jackie went with me.

"Amanda, there will be plenty of people you know in your class," Mom said. She took some hot clothes out of the dryer and started folding them. "Jackie Charles is not the only nice person in the world. And you don't have to be Jackie's shadow." I hated when she used that tone of voice with me. To make it even worse, she snapped a towel at my stomach. Ha, ha—she missed.

"You don't like Jackie!" I said. I was in a fighting mood, even though I knew there was no way I could win with Mom.

Mom took a long time folding one of Dad's golf shirts. "I like Jackie fine," she said. "But—"

I tuned out the rest of her speech—I'd heard it all before. Mom thought that I was missing out on making other good friends by sticking so close to Jackie. She finished talking and forced a stack of clothes into my hands. "Here. *Put them away.* I don't want to find them on top of your toy chest later."

"It's not a toy chest, it's a window seat," I said, and marched to my room. Dad built the toy chest for Laura, and now I had moved it beneath the window. I had put two little round pillows on top, which were supposed to make it look comfortable. It wasn't.

The rest of my room was kind of plain. I had twin beds with light blue bedspreads, a little table between the beds, and a dresser with a mirror over it. On the wall above the beds I had a Beatles poster that Laura gave me. It was a copy of the "Let It Be" album cover. I put up with John and Ringo so I could look at Paul and George. Especially George.

I went back to Mom, who had started ironing. "Why can't I go to private school, too?" I asked. "Don't you care about my education at all?"

Mom shot me a look as sharp as a slap in the face. "The private school you're so anxious to attend doesn't have any equipment, supplies, or even adequate facilities," she said. "Furthermore, I don't feel sorry for you at all. I'll tell you who I do feel sorry for. I feel sorry for the little ones who are being bused from the east side over here to your old school. Imagine being in first grade and having to ride miles away from home to go to school. If one of those little fellows gets sick, he'll be a pretty long way from home."

I remembered like it was yesterday how it felt to go off to school with my bus number written on a tag pinned to my shirt. Those little black kids would probably need a whole *map* pinned to their shirts. But I only felt sorry for them for about two seconds.

"But Jackie's my *best friend*," I said. "Don't you even care that I'll never get to see her? She'll forget all about me and find another best friend."

"You'll see Jackie on weekends, and afternoons, and in Sunday school, and during vacations," Mom said. She didn't even stop ironing to say that. "And Amanda, you know that I don't particularly care for this talk about *best* friends."

I knew that, all right. Mom thought it was better to have several good friends. But all the girls in books (like Anne of Green Gables, for example) had best friends. It had taken me a long time to get Jackie Charles as a best friend, and now everything was ruined. It made me wonder if Mom had talked the school system into desegregating just to separate me and Jackie.

What Mom didn't understand was that I *needed* Jackie. She was always the center of everything, and as her best friend that put *me* close to the center of everything. Jackie liked for everybody else to be just like her, only not as strong. She was a natural leader, and she loved telling everybody how to act, what to wear, who to like, and who to ignore. As her best friend, I could count on not being ignored, or laughed at, or talked about behind my back. That was a *very* valuable thing.

"This is a great opportunity," Mom said. "It's your chance to find out who *you* are, without Jackie telling you first." She ironed the collar of a shirt, then flipped the sleeve onto the ironing board and squirted some water out of a spray bottle on it. But the lecture wasn't over yet. "Change is going to happen," she said. "You have to learn to face it. Think of yourself as a pioneer, Amanda! Integration is going to change this country for the better, and you're a part of that. You can help make it happen."

So *that's* where Laura had gotten the pioneer line. Mom was still talking away. "It's always hard for pioneers. They have to face danger, and there's a fear of the unknown. Like the wagon trains heading west, not knowing if the Indians were going to attack, or if the winter snows would catch them by surprise." Mom's face was getting pink, either from talking or ironing, and the dark hair at her forehead was beginning to curl from the steam. "Lucky for you, there aren't any Indians, and if it snows, they'll cancel school," she smiled. She is even prettier than Laura, I think.

Then she got serious again. "Integration is an important step for us," she said. "It's time to stop talking about equality in this country and start really working to achieve it. Yes, you'll be changing schools, but the trick is to see the change as an opportunity to learn something new. And like I said, you can make a brand-new start. You can begin the school year being anything you want."

I thought about that. "Maybe I'll be a conductor," I said. I threw my head back and stood perfectly straight with my arms out, like a conductor standing in front of an orchestra.

"That's fine," Mom said. "That's a good leadership position. You're not a sheep, Amanda."

But maybe I really was a sheep, and happy to be one. I dropped my arms and slumped. "Mom, integration is fine with me. I don't care if we integrate the whole entire universe. The problem is, Jackie is my best friend, and I want to stay with her. So if I promise to do everything you tell me the minute you tell me, and to make all As and not read any more trashy books or *Mad* magazines, could I please go to private school with Jackie?"

It was a good thing Mom had an iron in her hand, otherwise I might have thought she had steam coming out her nose like a cartoon bull. "*No,* Amanda," she said in a calm, scary tone. "You are not going to private school, and we will wait to continue this discussion after supper, with your father."

Laura came out of her room and looked at us. "Take my advice, Little Bit," she said. "Run away while you still can."

I did.

CHAPTER 6

After supper I had to listen to Mom and Dad for thirty minutes. It was like I was a Ping-Pong ball that they kept hitting back and forth. As soon as one of them finished talking, the other started up, and I never had a chance to open my mouth.

Dad started it. "Amanda, your mom tells me that you've decided you want to go to private school this year. Why is that?"

I rolled my eyes. Everybody (even Laura) was looking at me like I was an exhibit at the state fair.

"Because Jackie is going to private school," I said. "I'd go to public school if Jackie would. I've already *told* Mom that it's not like I'm against integration or anything. I wish everybody would stop acting like there's something wrong with me."

Dad leaned back in his chair and looked at me. "I understand your feelings," he said, like he was doing me a big favor. "Now let me explain my feelings to you. I didn't grow up in North Carolina, you know . . ."

Dad grew up in Cherry Hill, New Jersey, where they eat *sauerkraut* instead of chili on hot dogs. And that wasn't the half of it. All of our friends called their parents "Mama" and "Daddy," but Laura and I said "Mom" and "Dad." It made us sound like Yankees.

"Things are different in Jersey," he said. "I grew up and went to school with blacks, and that's how it should be. I'm not saying everything was perfect, but at least blacks weren't harassed and their churches weren't bombed."

"Michael, what is your point?" Mom asked. She had a crease between her eyes, and I could tell she didn't like the way the conversation was going.

"My point, Jannette, is that here in the South, there's an even bigger responsibility to pay for the crimes of the past."

"I wish you wouldn't talk as though all of the racial problems of this country were centered in North Carolina," she said. "Anyway, Amanda, the point your father is trying to make is that we *do* have a responsibility to make things better. The law now says that Negro children can't be excluded from any public school. But the law didn't change the fact that in most places, Negroes live in one section of town and go to the schools in that section, while white children live in another section of town and go to the schools in that section. That's called *de facto* segregation—segregation is a fact, even though the courts have ruled that schools cannot be segregated."

De facto. It sounded like a musical direction. Like the word *fortissimo*, which means play really loud, or *pianissimo*, very softly.

Dad was still talking. "By making things better for black citizens, this country will be better for all of us. Everybody wins."

"Everybody wins except me," I said. "I still have to go to school without my best friend. I know you think that's not important, but it's important to me."

Mom sighed. "Amanda, I've told you. You'll still see Jackie a lot. We know how you feel, but we're trying to make you understand that you're doing something important, something that makes a difference."

"Well, I'm making a difference, and Laura's making a difference, I guess, but I don't see you and Dad doing anything to make a difference."

"We're trying to make a difference, too," Mom said. "We're voting for people who want to make things better for everybody. Your dad makes a difference at work, when he hires subcontractors based only on the bid they make on the job, not on who they are."

I looked at my dirty plate and counted the peas I hadn't eaten. There were seven of them. "Your life isn't turning upside down," I said. I raised my head and saw Mom and Dad looking at each other. Then Mom looked at me again.

"Your dad has made some sacrifices, too, Amanda," she said. "If he joined the country club, he could make more business contacts and entertain clients there. It would help his business a lot."

"Not to mention the fact that it's the most beautiful golf course this side of Myrtle Beach," Dad sighed.

"But the country club is segregated, so we didn't join."

I had always thought Dad *liked* playing golf at Woodhills Park, where they had picnic tables and a swimming pool and a putt-putt course. He had never complained about it.

"I'll tell you something else, Amanda," Mom said, "I

27

don't want you to grow up with the kind of guilt I've carried around with me." She stopped. "My family didn't treat Negroes badly at all, and they never said a word against them. A Negro family called Morrison lived right across the road from my daddy's farm, and every summer Daddy hired the Morrison kids to help me and your uncle Pete stake tomatoes."

Mom took a drink of iced tea. "Pleasant Springs was an amusement park about fifteen miles from your grandma Braverman's house. A friend of my daddy's ran it—Mr. Hill. Pleasant Springs had a lake for swimming, and a Ferris wheel and merry-go-round, and a couple of other rides. It wasn't half the size of Frontier Village, but when I was your age, Amanda, I thought it was wonderful. At least once every summer we used to take a picnic and stay all day. The summer I was fourteen, we went to Pleasant Springs right before time for the tomatoes to be staked, and as usual I had a great time. That next Monday we started on the tomatoes. Uncle Pete and one of the Morrison boys would put a stake behind a tomato plant, and Estelle Morrison and her little sister and I went along behind them, pulling the tomato vines up and tying them to the stakes with strips of old sheets. The whole time we worked I told Estelle about what fun it was to go to Pleasant Springs, and how I wished I could go there every day instead of having to tie up tomato plants. And Estelle smiled and nodded and agreed with me that that would be absolute heaven."

Mama stopped. She patted her glass with a napkin, then blotted the table where her glass had left a wet circle. "It didn't hit me until I'd gone back to the house and was sitting in the tub, trying to get the dirt and sweat off, that Estelle and her family weren't *allowed* in Pleasant Springs. I felt so stupid, and for the first time I began to see that things weren't right. Ten or twelve years later, Mr. Hill shut Pleasant Springs down. He shut it down so that it wouldn't have to be integrated."

Mom's eyes looked like they needed to be blotted with a napkin, too.

That did it. They had worn me down. I looked from Mom to Dad, then back to Mom. "Well, can you just tell me one thing?" I asked. "What am I supposed to say? Am I supposed to say 'Negro,' like Mom, or 'black,' like Dad?"

Laura answered. "Black," she said. "Mom isn't quite with it, yet. She's getting there, though."

I called Jackie as soon as I could escape. Everything was up to Jackie. She had to get her parents to change their minds. "*Beg* them," I told her. "Beg them until you're blue in the face. Pitch one of your biggest fits, like the one you pitched over having a horseback riding birthday party last year. They'll give in, if you just *try*."

"I don't think so," Jackie said. I could hear her yawning over the telephone.

"You've got to try," I said. It wasn't like me to be so pushy, but I was desperate. "It's going to be great," I said. "We're like pioneers, like the first man to walk on the moon. We'll be the first white kids to go to East Windsor Elementary School! This is history, happening right now where we are. Come on, Jackie! Start working on your mom and dad tomorrow morning, first thing, and by the time school starts, everything will be all right. Just say, 'I want to go to school with Amanda. I don't want to go to a stupid new private school that doesn't have proper facilities or supplies or even a cafeteria.' Jackie, I know you can make them change their minds."

Jackie yawned again. "I don't want to," she said.

I sat there for a little while, listening to the faraway telephone line static. "You're prejudiced," I said.

"No, I'm not," she said. "I just don't want to go to a school that's not even *my* school."

"Oh, like the private school that just started up this week is *your* school," I said. "It's *nobody's* school."

"Yeah? But you'd go there in a heartbeat, if you could," she said.

Well, she had me there.

CHAPTER 7

Orientation was on Saturday, August 21, from one until three o'clock. Mom and Dad let me sit between them in the front seat on the way to East Windsor. "This is more or less the way your bus will go every day," Mom said. "You'll get on the Interstate . . ."

"As we are doing *now*," Dad said. He pretended to shift gears, even though the car was an automatic. Usually that made me laugh.

". . . and from there it'll be about thirty minutes to the school."

When we got off the highway, East Windsor High School was on the right. Laura's high school in our part of town was built all on one level, with lots of windows and square panels painted bright colors—red, turquoise, orange, and blue. It almost looked like modern art. This high school was a big old brick building that looked like it had been soaking in the air pollution too long. (There were some factories with pretty big smokestacks not too far away.)

East Windsor Elementary School was a little bit further from the highway. It looked better than the high school, because there were only two floors, and all the windows had

stuff in them, like numbers cut out of construction paper
($7 \times 9 = ?$) and flowers. It looked like the teachers had really
made an effort.

Still, the school looked big, and I felt smaller than the
smallest bug that crawled. Well, no, actually I *wished* I was
smaller than the smallest bug that crawled. "We don't even
know where we're supposed to go," I said.

"Yes, we do," Mom said. She had a letter in her hand.
"We're supposed to meet in the cafeteria."

"Oh, yeah, like I really know where the cafeteria is," I
said. I was beginning to get mad at everyone. When I got
out of the car behind Mom, I slammed the door extra hard.

"You're right!" Dad said. He grabbed my arm like he was
terrified. "What should we do? I'm sure they won't have
anyone there to show us where the cafeteria is, and I'm sure
that all these people around us aren't going there, too. Do
you suppose we'll just have to wander around this parking
lot for the rest of our lives?"

"You're not funny," I said, shaking his hand off my arm.
Sometimes I understood exactly how Ted felt when I wanted
to kiss his little head and he wanted to be put down. "It
smells like tobacco," I said.

"Galt Brothers Tobacco Company is only about three
blocks away," Dad told me. "I like the smell, though."

So did I. It smelled sweet and strange, like I imagined
frankincense and myrrh might smell.

As we walked up the front steps of the school, there were
people with name tags on to direct us, and there were big
yellow signs that pointed the way to the cafeteria.

In the cafeteria, a tall black man introduced himself as Mr.

Harrison, the principal of East Windsor Elementary School, and he introduced the school secretary, Mrs. Leland. Then he turned toward the man sitting next to Mrs. Leland and said, "This is our head maintenance man, Albert Deane. But around here we call him Sporty."

Mr. Harrison talked about some of the changes that had been made to the school because of desegregation.

"The first- and second-grade rooms have been completely remodeled to accommodate the older students who will now be using them," he said. "We have expanded the playgrounds, and we've added a team-building obstacle course donated by a local corporation. The playgrounds aren't on the planned tour for today, but anyone who would like may go outside and take a look around before heading home. However, all students need to stay with their parents. I know how you parents can get when you're let loose. Now I'm going to let Mrs. Leland tell you about the school tour."

We were divided into smaller groups for tours of the school, depending on our grade. There was such a crowd of people, and I was so nervous, that I didn't see anybody I knew. Not a single, solitary person. I stayed so close to Mom that I stepped on her heel and pulled her shoe off, giving her what we called a flat tire. We saw the library, the gymnasium, some classrooms, and the principal's office. After her third flat tire, Mom made me walk in front of her.

"This reminds me of the school I went to in Cherry Hill," Dad said as we headed back to the cafeteria. "It had shiny brown linoleum on the floors, too. Yeah, this really takes me back."

"You must have grown up in the first century B.C.," I said.

"Did you *see* that library?" I whispered, so no one else could hear me complain. "It was so little and dark. I bet they don't have any good books here. Aren't we supposed to turn left here to get to the cafeteria? I'm never going to be able to find my way around. I'll flunk sixth grade just because I can't find my *room*."

Back at the cafeteria, I found out that my teacher's name was Miss Gohagan, and her classroom was Room 23. Mr. Harrison told us that for the rest of the orientation time we were to go to our classrooms and meet our teachers, and once we'd had all our questions answered we could feel free to leave at any time.

"But don't hesitate to knock on my door, if you have any questions or concerns," he said. "I'll be down the hall in my office. I'd be happy to talk with you." Then he smiled and said, "Okay, now, get to your classes before I write you all up and start handing out demerits." The parents were the only ones who laughed.

"Okay," Mom said, fumbling with her map. "Room twenty-three. That must be on the second floor, right?"

"No, Mom, it's on the first floor," I told her. "We go down this hall past the library, and then left down the main hall."

"Oh," Mom said. "Gee, I thought you would *never* be able to find your way around."

We found Room 23 and sat down near the front. I was afraid to look around to see if I knew anyone, but right after we sat down Darlene Jeffries came in. Darlene had been in my class every year since first grade, and she had always been the *only* black kid in my class.

34

Darlene was with her mother, and they sat in the row behind us. I turned around and waved, and Darlene smiled. "Hey, Amanda," she whispered.

Miss Gohagan introduced herself and spelled her name out on the blackboard. She was young, with long straight blond hair and a smile that went way up on the sides. "I'm not going to keep you here long," she said. "I just want to run over our curriculum very quickly, then take a class picture. After that, I'll be available for any questions you may have."

Miss Gohagan talked about what textbooks we'd be using for math, science, and social studies. "There is special emphasis on current events in this year's sixth-grade curriculum," she said. "I am so excited about this, and I hope you sixth-graders will be, too. Each of you will be given a journal like this one on the first day of school. When you see a news story that catches your eye, you can put it in your journal. When a topic *really* grabs your interest, you may also write a paragraph or two stating your own opinion on the story. The journals will be used for interviewing fellow students and for recording any thoughts you may have on class activities, current events, or books you read. Parents, as you can see, the journals will incorporate reading skills, writing skills, and social studies."

Miss Gohagan put the journal on top of the stack of textbooks on her desk. "Now, if all of the students would please come stand in front of the blackboard, we'll take that class picture."

Miss Gohagan was young, but she knew how to organize people. In about two minutes we were all lined up. "Let's put our taller people in the back, then a row of shorter peo-

35

ple, then a row of people squatting down. Okay, I've already checked this out. We have to stay within the pieces of tape I've put on the floor, or everyone won't be in the picture. All my people on the ends of rows look down now and make sure your feet are inside the tape."

We shuffled together a little closer. I bumped shoulders with a tall black girl on one side and a skinny white boy on the other. He made a face like he hated being touched by a girl, but I could tell it was nothing personal. Miss Gohagan went to the middle of the classroom and looked through her camera. The parents in the front rows moved aside. "That looks wonderful," Miss Gohagan said.

"Why don't you get in the picture, too," Dad said, "and I'll be the photographer?"

Miss Gohagan was thrilled. She squeezed in on one end of the group, and Dad said, "Okay, say 'I love school.'" That didn't work, so he said, "All right, all right, say 'cheese.'"

We all said, "cheese," and the flash went off. As soon as it flashed, we all ran for our seats. There's nothing worse than rubbing bare arms with a bunch of people you've never seen before in your life. I had a feeling I was going to feel that way for the whole entire school year.

CHAPTER 8

"Before we leave," Mom said, "let's meet your new piano teacher, Mrs. Gandy. She's in room B-ten."

Mrs. Gandy's room was in the basement of the school. The hallway was awfully long and dark. The lights overhead were sort of dim, and the only other light was from the sunlight coming through the windows into the classrooms, then through the open doors to the hall. The door to the art room was open. It was the size of two normal classrooms, and as we walked past it smelled like plaster and wet paint. Sporty came out of another room with a mop in his hand.

"Good afternoon, Sporty," Dad said.

"Hey, there, Sporty," he answered. "Welcome to the East Windsor Elementary School." Sporty had a low, relaxed voice. He was skinny, with some gray in his hair. He wore tan work pants and a matching tan short-sleeved shirt, and he had a pack of Galt Brothers Cherokee cigarettes in his shirt pocket, the kind with the Indian chief's head on the top of the pack.

Sporty nodded at me. "You must be going to see Mrs. Gandy."

"Yes, I take piano," I said.

"Well, well. Nice to see you all this fine day." Sporty looked at me again. "You gonna do just fine there, Sporty. I'll be seeing you around."

We watched Sporty move on down the hall. "I guess he's Sporty, and so is everybody else," Dad said.

Now we could hear piano music. The closer we got to B-10, the louder the music became.

When we went in the door, Mrs. Gandy had her back to us. She sat on a rolling piano stool and rolled as she played, anchored only to the foot pedal. She was a tall, big black woman, with powerful arms.

"Wow," I said. Mrs. Gandy used her entire body to play the piano, and I really only used my hands.

Mrs. Gandy finished her song with a flourish, and as soon as she had brought her hands off the keys Dad started to applaud. Mrs. Gandy whirled around on her stool, smiling. She had short hair styled so that it flipped up a little on both sides. "Thank you, sir, thank you," she said. "I'm May Gandy, and I teach piano and music appreciation." She held out her hand.

"Michael Adams," Dad said, shaking hands. "This is my wife, Jannette, and our daughter, Amanda. Amanda is signed up for piano lessons."

"Wonderful!" Mrs. Gandy said. "Are you a beginner, Amanda, or have you been taking piano for a while?"

"I've had four years," I said.

Mrs. Gandy turned back to the keyboard, and while she talked she played soft background music that rose and fell with her voice. "You'll be staying after school on Monday afternoons for piano," she said. She had a small calendar on top of her piano, and she consulted it while she played. "Now, you won't come in on the first day of school, and the Monday after that one is Labor Day. So your first lesson will be on September thirteenth." She finished one last bar of music and swung back around.

"For that first lesson, Amanda, I want you to bring in a piece of music to play for me, so I can see where we stand. Bring in anything you like. Now, Mama," she said, turning to my mom, "are you going to be picking Amanda up on piano days? Do you want to come in and sit with us, or will you wait for Amanda out front?"

"Oh, I'll wait out front," Mom said. "I don't want to get in the way."

"That's just what I like to hear," Mrs. Gandy said. "Well, Amanda, I'll see you here on September thirteenth."

The sound of Mrs. Gandy's playing followed us down the hall. I wanted to run back and ask her something, but I was afraid of sounding stupid. I wanted to say, "Mrs. Gandy, you hear it, too, don't you?" See, most of the time I hear music playing in my head, and it sort of goes with whatever mood I'm in at the time. The way Mrs. Gandy played, I thought she heard music in her head, too. And it sounded like she was usually in a *terrific* mood.

CHAPTER 9

On our way to church on Sunday we drove past the future home of Jackie's new school: the New Canaan Academy, at the New Canaan Christian Church.

"Where are they going to put everybody?" I asked. "Will it be like a one-room schoolhouse, and everybody will meet in the sanctuary?"

"They'll probably use the Sunday school rooms," Mom said. "Although how they're going to manage that little juggling act, I couldn't tell you. Can you imagine?" she asked Dad. "School five days a week, then Sunday school, and all the supplies and tables and chairs to be shuffled around. What a nightmare."

Mom seemed determined to criticize everything about the new school. When she didn't like something, she didn't like it a lot.

When I got to my Sunday school class, I sat next to Jackie. We had wooden chairs around two tables in our class. Jackie and I always sat at the one farthest away from Miss Elaine, our Sunday school teacher.

"We had our orientation yesterday," I told Jackie. "That school's so old, my dad thought he was back at *his* elementary school."

41

"Aren't you going to New Canaan Academy?" Heather Baker asked me. "I am. I thought our whole Sunday school class would be going there."

Sitting beside Jackie, I was braver than I would be on my own. "No, I'm going to East Windsor Elementary," I said. I tried to look and sound annoyed that she had interrupted us.

"East Windsor Elementary!" Jackie laughed. "EWE!"

"Ewwwwwww," I said, like something smelled bad. "That pretty much says it all about old East Windsor Elementary."

"Girls, settle down back there," Miss Elaine said. "Turn to page twenty-two in your *Bible Discoveries* book. Page twenty-two."

Miss Elaine decided to go around the room asking questions. It was her sneaky way of finding out who had read their lesson and who hadn't.

"Oh, no," I whispered to Jackie. "I didn't read my lesson!"

"The answer's always 'Jesus,' " she said. "Or 'love one another.' It's easy."

"What if it's a *fact* question?" I asked her. "Like 'Where does today's story take place?' "

"Say 'the Holy Land,' " she said, right in the middle of a yawn. I started laughing—I couldn't help it. There's no place like church for making me get the giggles.

"Girls," Miss Elaine said, "settle down, now. Amanda, can you give us the answer to that last question?"

"Say 'Jesus,' " Jackie whispered.

"I think the answer is Jesus," I said, but I guess it was wrong because Miss Elaine made Jackie go and sit on the other side of the room so we couldn't talk and laugh together.

We got to sit together during the worship service, though, and we played Hangman on the backs of our bulletins. We could play without talking at all, just by writing down the letters we were guessing on one side of the page. The only problem was, if the sermon was extra long, we ran out of space to play and had to sit and listen instead. Usually we grabbed a couple of extra bulletins to be sure we didn't run out of space. I didn't mind the preaching too much, really—it was a good time to sit and think about things, and I sometimes spent the extra time planning my wedding. I'd plan where to put the flowers, and the candles, and the bridesmaids and flower girl and ring bearer, and sometimes Laura was my maid of honor, but usually Jackie was, and all the bridesmaids wore dark purple dresses, because dark purple was Jackie's favorite color.

"Reverend Collins is impossible," Mom said as we got in the car to go home. "The man wouldn't take a stand on an issue if . . . if it were a *rug.* I keep waiting for him to say *something* about desegregation, but all he does is smile and smile."

Just then Reverend Collins walked past us on his way to his car, and Mom smiled and waved at him. He smiled real big and waved back. Mom was right, he did smile too much.

Dad laughed. "Well, Jannette, his biggest ambition is to be everybody's friend. He doesn't want to alienate anybody in the congregation. It sure is lucky for him that his kids are

43

already grown up and out of school. Anyways I keep telling you that I'm perfectly willing to change churches. We could always go back to my family's Lutheran heritage."

Mom sighed. "I don't want to have to learn all new hymns," she said. She laughed, sort of. "Still, it may come to that. Or maybe we could find a more enlightened Baptist church."

"Oh, that's perfect!" I said. "Yeah, let's go to another church, too, and then I won't have any friends there, either."

Mom put her chin on her left shoulder and frowned at me. "Jackie's mother asked me why you weren't going to private school," she said. "Amanda, did you tell her to talk to me about it?"

"Of course not," I said. "*I* don't talk to Mrs. Charles. Jackie probably asked her to do it."

"The woman is absolutely infuriating," Mom said. "She comes up to me and in this terribly confidential tone says, 'Jannette, Jackie is *so* unhappy that she and Amanda won't be in school together this year, and I know you don't want her riding clear across town in a *bus*. I thought I'd let you know that New Canaan has a tuition payment plan. I'd be happy to send you information on it.' "

"Anyway," Dad said, clearing his throat real loud, "speaking of hymns, I thought the choice of songs was rather interesting this morning."

"Why?" I asked. "What'd we sing?"

"If you would pay attention in church, you'd know," Mom said.

I looked in my bulletin. "We sang 'Amazing Grace,' ' In Christ There Is No East or West . . .' "

44

"That's the one," Dad said.

"Oh. I get it. Like East Windsor and West Windsor, huh?" I said. That made Dad laugh, and even Mom stopped frowning, so I considered that I had done my Christian duty for the day by cheering everybody up.

The day before school began, Mom took me to get my hair trimmed. "Just a little," she said. "To get rid of the frizzies."

She took me to Frederica's House of Beauty. The lady who cut my hair wasn't Frederica, though. Her name was Alice. She was chewing a wad of gum and breathing out a strong grape smell.

"Just a light trim," Mom told her.

But Alice didn't seem to hear too well. She chopped off about three inches. She started at the back, so I didn't realize what was happening until it was too late. "This cut will really show off your face, Miranda," she said, and spun me around to the mirror.

Miranda wasn't my name, and I couldn't believe that was my face in the mirror. Jackie and I weren't going to be able to dress up like Siamese twins at Halloween this year.

CHAPTER 10

The next morning, everybody in my family tried to act like it was a normal day. But I could barely choke down my Cheerios.

"I like this guy," Dad said. He waved the newspaper at Mom, who had her elbows on the table while she drank a cup of coffee. "This Walter Cunningham, he's a good guy. I like him." Walter Cunningham was the editor of the Windsor *Observer*. Dad agreed with almost every column he wrote. Walter Cunningham was for desegregation.

"He's a Southerner, too, Dad," Laura said.

Now he shook the newspaper in Laura's face. *"Educated at Princeton,"* he said. "You girls know what state Princeton's in, doncha?"

"New Jersey," we said together.

Dad folded the newspaper and snapped it against the table, and he looked so happy and proud that we all laughed.

I went to the end of our driveway to wait for my bus. Laura came with me, even though her bus came later. Since she was a senior, she would still be attending her old school. Laura was perfectly calm, as usual. She was swinging her purse in a circle. It was a striped drawstring bag with a stiff round bottom. She wore bell-bottom blue jeans and a tight, sleeveless white shirt that zipped up the front. The zipper had a big metal ring dangling from it. She is the most in-fashion person I know.

"Do you think I wore the right thing for the first day of school?" I asked her. I was wearing my white short-sleeved peasant blouse with red pants. I also wore brown sandals.

"*Certainement,*" she said, squinting at me carefully. "You can't go wrong in those pants. You know what, though? You need just one more little touch . . ." And she took off her own silver bangle bracelet and handed it to me. "Put this on your right arm," she said.

I slid the bracelet over my hand, then put my hand on my hip.

"That's it," Laura said. "Perfect."

"I promise not to lose it," I said. I opened my purse and looked inside. "Did I forget anything?" But it was too late to start wondering, because my bus pulled up.

"Relax, Little Bit," Laura said. "Try to have fun."

Try to have fun? In the old days, Jackie would have already been on the bus, and she'd have been waving for me to come sit with her. I sat in the first empty seat I saw and slid over to the window.

I thought back to my first day of real school, when I'd started first grade. Back then Jackie had lived just two houses down the road from us. That was before her parents moved to a bigger house several miles away. Our moms had fixed it up so that we would get on the bus together and look after each other. I had never ridden a school bus without Jackie.

I was glad to see that *some* people from my old school were going to the new school, even if they weren't going to be in my class. Gordon Grahame, a fifth-grader, sat next to me.

"It feels weird, taking the superhighway to school," Gordon said.

The scenery did go by a lot slower than it did in a car.

"Hey, Amanda," he said, "are you scared?"

"No," I said. "And there's no reason for you to be scared, either."

"I don't know, the way everybody's acting, this must be a really big deal. I think it's dangerous, even."

I gave him a look like the ones my mother is always giving me. "Oh, for heaven's sake, Gordon," I said, "do you really think we'd be packed into a bus and sent downtown if it were dangerous? Anyway, my dad says we're really lucky, because there hasn't even been any demonstrating against desegregation here. It's been a 'perfectly calm transition,' he said."

Gordon's eyes bugged out. "Demonstrating?" he whispered. "Tear gas?"

My stomach knotted as it hit me that not only was I going to school without Jackie, I was also going into a strange new world. What if all the rules were different? What if it blew up in my face? Strange things were going on all over the United States of America. Everybody was mad about something—the war in Vietnam, or women getting liberated. Sometimes even Mom and Dad argued about women's lib (with Laura joining in), and once Dad had told them both, "Awww, keep your bras on." I had thought that was pretty funny. But now that I thought about it, what was happening in the real world wasn't funny. Out there the arguments sometimes turned into riots and demonstrations and tear gas, like Gordon had said. I remembered Laura crying over a newspaper picture of a college boy lying face down in the street, with his arms tucked underneath his body and all of his blood running by the curb. And there was a girl beside him, screaming and waving her arms. I hated that picture. I hated that picture.

I took a deep breath and turned to look out the window. I remembered other pictures I'd hated, pictures of police dogs jumping at black kids, and pictures of a black girl having to walk past crowds of screaming people while guards held them back so she could get through. She was carrying a notebook and a pencil. It was her first day of school, too.

The ninth- and tenth-graders on my bus got off first at East Windsor High School, and then the bus parked next to my new school. As I walked up to the front doors, I felt like I glowed in the dark, I was so white.

A black girl ran up to me and got right in my face. I looked for a teacher, but the only one I saw was busy telling a group of kids where to go. The black girl stared at me. "You need me to show you where the bathroom is?" she asked.

"Not right now," I said. "Thanks, though."

"Okay," she said, and she ran up to some other girl, I guess to ask her if *she* needed to know where the bathroom was.

That girl seemed friendly, but I still wondered if these

black kids were mad because all us white kids were coming to school there. I looked around. It was mostly white kids getting off the buses, and there was Mr. Harrison, the principal. He was directing traffic. In his short-sleeved white shirt and red tie, he looked big and solid and safe, like somebody's dad.

But I couldn't stay out in the parking lot all day, and as I walked into the school I thought about the Twenty-third Psalm: "Yea, though I walk through the valley of the shadow of death, I will fear no evil. I will fear no evil. Surely goodness and mercy shall follow me all the days of my life, and I will fear no evil."

But no matter how many times I thought those words, I couldn't stop hearing Bach's Toccata and Fugue in D Minor in my head. I call it "Tornado in D," because one part sounds like a tornado is coming, and it's heading right for *you.*

CHAPTER 11

The hallways were full of strangers. I kept looking down at my red pants, so I almost didn't even see Amy Voorhees and Jennifer Reddenfield. Amy had been in my room for the past two years, and Jennifer went to my church.

"Amanda!" Amy said, and I was so happy to see somebody I knew that I hugged her. "Are you in Miss Gohagan's class? So am I," Amy said. "Jennifer's in Mr. Gordon's class. I missed orientation. Let's sit together, okay?"

"Sure," I said, trying to be cool. But inside I felt great. I liked Amy. She wasn't Jackie, but she was all right.

"I'm so glad you didn't go to private school," I told her.

"Well, to tell you the truth, I kinda wish I was," she said. She made a face. "I wanted to be with people I know, but Daddy says my education is more important than anything else, and he thinks the private schools are terrible. He and Mama fought about it."

Miss Gohagan was waiting in the classroom, smiling like she was thrilled to be there. "Good morning," she said, once the second bell had rung and everybody was sitting down. "Those of you who were able to come for orientation will remember that I'm Miss Gohagan. I want to begin by giving each of you a class picture."

She passed out copies. It had turned out clear, anyway. I looked stupid (I always look stupid in pictures), but there were other people who looked stupider, so that made me feel better.

"Now, in order to make my life a little easier, I'm going to assign seats alphabetically. So everyone stand up and move over by the doorway. As I call your name, come find your seat."

Amy and I looked at each other, and I wanted to cry. You can't get much farther apart, alphabetically, than Adams and Voorhees.

"I hate her," Amy whispered. "I already hate her." We shuffled over toward the doorway with the rest of the class. There were as many black kids as there were white kids, and we all sort of clumped together.

"Amanda Adams," Miss Gohagan said, pointing to the first seat of the first row, beside the windows. I sat down.

"Henry Bailey."

Henry Bailey was a tall black boy with short hair. He wore a light blue short-sleeved shirt. He had a crooked, cocky grin, and as he came and sat down behind me he said loudly, "That's me, Henry B."

Miss Gohagan smiled back at him. "Marcella Bailey," she said, and the tall black girl I'd stood next to in the class picture came forward. Her hair was pulled back in a short ponytail, and she had bangs that curved like parentheses over her forehead.

"Miss Gohagan," she said in a soft voice, "I want to go by my middle name."

Miss Gohagan looked at her list and made a note on it. "All right, *Joy* Bailey. Any relation to Henry B?"

"He's my brother," Joy said. She took her seat behind Henry.

"Don't go claiming kin with me," Henry said.

I heard a couple of other names I knew from my old school as Miss Gohagan assigned our seats, but they were boys (Scott Monroe and John Williams). After we all sat down, Miss Gohagan passed around a big calendar so we could write our names on our birthdays. While we did that, Miss Gohagan looked through a booklet the size of a book of piano music. It had a red cover with no writing on the outside. Miss Gohagan closed the booklet and stood up.

"This is a rather unusual school year," she said. "Obviously, there have been a lot of changes. But one thing has not changed, and that is that here we are, a bunch of different people, thrown together by chance in a schoolroom, and it's our job to learn as much as we possibly can during the next nine months. One of the interesting things about this school year is that, in addition to learning math, science, and history, we have a unique opportunity to learn about each other. I want us to make the most of this opportunity.

"You know that this is the first year of desegregation in Windsor County, North Carolina. It's the beginning of a new era for us all. Those of you who were here for orientation already know that we are going to record our own history by keeping journals this school year of current events, class activities, and personal interviews. When you are all old enough to have children of your own, they will have grown up in a world that was never segregated. The journal of your sixth-grade year will give you something unique to share with them. So I'm warning you now—in twenty years I'm going to track you all down, just to make sure that you still have your journals!

"We'll talk about the journals in more detail later. Today, we're going to go outside to do something kind of special that I think will help us get acquainted. Please follow me, in an orderly fashion, and I'll explain more when we get outside."

Amy and I got back together as we followed Miss Gohagan outside across a ball field to a little area with trees growing all around. There was a sort of obstacle course set up, with a high wall in one place and a log hanging from chains between two trees, and a kind of rope ladder that was strung between a platform and another tree.

Miss Gohagan stood in front of the wall and turned to look at us. She had brought her red booklet with her. "This is more than just an obstacle course," she said. "It's a team-building course. It's designed to help you learn that you need each other, that you need to work together as a team to be successful. So the first thing I want to discuss with you, briefly, is the fundamentals of teamwork. Can anyone help me out? What makes a team?"

No one said anything. We were probably the least likely team you could possibly find anywhere. Jackie Charles and I were a team.

"All right, I'll tell you," Miss Gohagan said. "The fundamentals of teamwork are compromise, cooperation, tact, and leadership. You need a strong leader to pull you together, but a leader isn't enough. You also must have the courtesy and brains to work things out together, even if you don't always agree on how things should be done. To successfully complete the obstacles on this course, you are going to have to elect a leader who can pull you together, but then you have to learn each other's strong points and weaknesses. You must learn to use the strengths to make up for the weaknesses. And you must learn to trust each other. Are there any questions? All right, then, the first thing you must do is select a leader. You discuss it among yourselves and then let me know what you decide." She walked over to the swinging log and sat on it.

Henry Bailey immediately took over. "I'm the oldest," he said, "so I'll be the leader."

"Yeah, you the oldest, all right," a girl named Gaylyn Graves said scornfully. She sat at the very back of our row. "Anybody who has to repeat sixth grade sure is going to be the oldest."

A couple of students snickered, but Henry stared at them till they shut up. "Now, what I'm saying is, I don't play. I *know* how to get the job done. I'm a natural-born leader, and I say vote me in and let's move on." His voice was becoming louder and more bossy with each word. He wasn't making a very good impression.

I wasn't the only one who thought so. "Oh, Henry," his sister said in a soft voice, "be still."

Henry whirled on her. "What you talking about 'be still?' I'll 'be still' you, girl. And that's about what you are, too—a

55

Beastle." Henry seemed pleased with himself for coming up with that. "Yes, I believe I'll be calling you Beastle from now on," he said. "And since I'm the leader, I'll make everybody else call you Beastle, too!"

Gaylyn Graves said, "Marcella, don't you let him call you names." But Henry's sister shook her head and didn't say anything else. I was glad that *I* hadn't done anything to draw Henry's attention.

Miss Gohagan walked back over. "I hope all this discussion means that you've elected a leader."

"*I'm* the leader," Henry announced.

"Did you have a vote?" Miss Gohagan asked. "No? Well, before we make Henry the leader by default, do I hear any other nominations or recommendations?"

"I say we let the man with the badge be the leader," Darlene Jeffries said, pointing her head toward a quiet black boy who wore a hall monitor's sash and badge.

"David, it looks like you've been nominated," Miss Gohagan said. "So the candidates are Henry Bailey and David Morgan. All those in favor of David Morgan, please raise your right hand."

Everyone except Henry Bailey voted for David Morgan.

"Well, David, it looks like you're it," Miss Gohagan said. "Henry, I think your politicking could use a little more tact and courtesy. Maybe you weren't listening to me earlier when I explained that cooperation and courtesy are essential to success. The mark of a great team is how well they are able to work together, and without those two qualities, no group is going to be able to make it for long. Now, here are the rules for your first problem."

56

David Morgan stepped forward, and Henry rolled his eyes in disgust. *"Badge* don't make no leader," he grumbled.

"I just loves a man in uniform," Darlene said. She caught my eye, and we tried not to laugh.

Darlene bent her head toward me and whispered, "Some of these girls told me he saved a five-year-old boy from drowning in a swimming pool last summer. He's a genuine, one-hundred-percent hero."

I looked at David again. He had eyes that crinkled up into slits when he smiled, and he wore his hair short. I'd have liked to talk to him about the rescue, but I felt shy. Maybe I could get Darlene to ask him.

The first obstacle was to get everyone up on the log that was hanging between the two trees and stay there for a full fifteen seconds without the log moving. It sounded easy, but it wasn't.

"You've got five minutes," Miss Gohagan said. "If anyone is left standing on the ground at the end of five minutes, or if the log is still swinging, it means you're all dead. Understand? Your very lives are at stake. Okay, class—*Go!*"

What happened next was pretty much a big disaster. David didn't lead, Henry never shut up, and nobody would cooperate anyway. It all ended with Henry pushing somebody, and then all the boys sort of divided into two groups. All of us girls stood to the side and watched as the white boys went on one side and the black boys went on the other. They just stood there staring each other down, while "Tornado in D" started pounding in my head.

"I want to go home," Amy whispered.

So did I.

CHAPTER 12

———————

"Time," Miss Gohagan said. She looked up from her stopwatch. "Well, my friends, you're all dead. Let's see if we have any better luck with the Wall."

Either she didn't notice the tension in the air, or she decided to ignore it. Anyway, as we followed her over to the Wall everybody got mixed up again, so it didn't look so much like a race riot was about to happen right there next to the East Windsor Elementary School.

The Wall looked strange in the middle of the trees, and it was really, really high and blank. We just stood there and stared at it. Miss Gohagan looked in her booklet. "The Wall is ten feet tall on this front side," she said. "Now come around here and let's look at the back."

At the back was a platform built up a little over halfway to the top. "The point is," Miss Gohagan said, "to figure out how to get everyone from the other side to this side by going over the Wall. There aren't any rules—you can get people over in any way that is safe. But you only have six minutes to do it. So why don't you guys take a look at it, think about it awhile, and decide how you're going to accomplish that. Let me know when you're ready, and I'll start the timer." She walked away and sat on the swinging log.

Henry Bailey was about to bust to tell us how this should be handled, and since David Morgan wasn't doing anything much, we started to listen to him. It was easier to listen to Henry than to ignore him. "There's not but one way to handle this thing," he was saying. He was talking to David Morgan, but we all paid attention. "We got to get the biggest people over there first, while there's a lot of people on this side to do the helping. See what I'm saying?"

Well, it did make sense, so Henry told Miss Gohagan we were ready and David Morgan made everybody line up like we had for the school picture, and David and Henry boosted the biggest boys over the Wall. They landed on the platform on the other side and then jumped off.

All the biggest boys were over the Wall before it dawned on Henry that some of them should stay on the platform to give the others a hand up. That helped, but we still weren't making much progress.

Miss Gohagan called time. There were still eight people not yet over the Wall, including Henry. "We're dead!" he said. "We're dead, and I don't know why. But I'm going to find out why, Miss Gohagan," he said as we walked back to the classroom. "We'll get her right next time. To be sure we will."

When I went back to my bus after school, I saw my piano teacher, Mrs. Gandy. She was on afternoon bus duty, and she had a list of which bus everybody should be on. Kids were lined up to talk to her.

"Now, what's your name, son?" she asked. It was Gordon Grahame. Trust Gordon not to remember his bus number.

"You're on number one-twelve," Mrs. Gandy told him. "Girls, don't be shoving and pushing! I promise you these buses are not going to leave until every last one of you is sitting on the one that goes right by your house. What's your name, sugar?"

I walked with Gordon to the bus. "I panicked," he said. "I *thought* our bus was one-twelve, but when I saw everybody checking their number, I figured I better check mine, too."

I slid into a seat and put my head against the window. It had been a long day, and I was tired. I closed my eyes, and for the whole long bus ride everything that had happened during the first day of school played back in my head like it was a movie. There had been many dangers, toils, and snares, like that one verse of "Amazing Grace." I thought about the words, and then changed them a little:

Through many dangers, toils, and snares
I have already come.
'Twas the bus that brought me safe thus far
And the bus will take me home.

"What are you smiling for?" Gordon asked me. He was sitting in front of me, but he was turned completely around in his seat. "Don't tell me you *liked* school!"

No, I didn't like it. But now that Day One was out of the way and I was on my way home, I felt almost like the pioneer that Mom and Laura had called me.

*   *   *

"How did school go today, Hotshot?" Dad asked. We were eating lasagna and garlic bread.

"It went okay." I was trying to act brave and depressed at the same time. Nobody seemed to notice.

Dad turned to Laura. "Any problems at your school, Miss Laura?"

"Just the usual confusion over where you're supposed to be when," Laura said.

"Who wants to help make chocolate chip cookies?" Mom asked, looking straight at me.

I loved everything about chocolate chip cookies. Mom was trying to make up for the fact that I had to go to school without Jackie. I stirred so hard that my wooden spoon broke off. But Mom said she didn't think we got any splinters in the dough, so we kept making cookies.

Mom had put my class picture on the refrigerator. She said it was a miracle that everybody had their eyes open.

Jackie called right after we put the first pan of cookies in the oven. New Canaan Academy wasn't going to start until after Labor Day weekend.

"I've been so bored all day," she said. I felt better. She had missed me!

"You can come over here and eat cookies," I said.

Jackie walked in the back door just as the first batch of cookies came out.

"Your hair!" she yelled. I hadn't seen her since my trim.

I tossed my head, trying to pretend it was all my own idea. "Don't you like it? Your hair would look good cut like this, too."

62

"You could sell Dutch Boy paint," she said.

"Get the milk," I told her. Mom went to the pantry to dig out the wire cooling rack.

"How was EWE?" Jackie asked, opening the refrigerator door. She stopped when she saw my class picture. "Who is that strange person?" she asked, pointing to the Bailey girl. In the picture she was leaning forward and staring into the camera, and she was so tall and skinny that she did look strange.

"They call her Beastle," I said in a haunted-house voice. I knew I was being mean, but I wanted to make Jackie laugh. Anyway, in the picture she *did* look like a Beastle. Big, ugly, quiet Beastle. A little whisper of guilt bothered me, but I was so glad somebody else had been nicknamed Beastle and not me. Maybe if *I* called her Beastle, nobody would have a chance to call *me* anything nasty. Sort of like a lucky charm.

"Beastle!" Jackie shrieked, and she laughed so hard her headband fell off her head.

"Her real name is Marcella," I said. "But she wants to be called Joy."

Jackie gave me one of her sharpest looks. "Her real name is *Beastle*," she said. "I love it!"

I held up my right hand like I was swearing in court to tell the whole truth. "I will never call her anything except Beastle. Actually, the whole entire *school* is a Beastle," I added, but Mom came in with the rack, so I shut up and started scraping cookies off the pan.

"There are only *five* white girls in your class?" Jackie said loudly. She was still examining my class picture.

"Amy Voorhees wasn't there for orientation, so she's not in

the picture," I said. "I was glad to see her this morning, let me tell you."

"Amy *Voorhees* goes to your school? Her dad's a doctor—I know *she* could afford to go to private school."

Mom banged the cooling rack on the counter.

I didn't tell Jackie that Amy's dad thought the private schools were terrible.

We took our cookies and milk into the living room. "I know you were scared," Jackie said. "Were there fights and stuff?" Her eyes shone.

"Nooo," I said, thinking about the race riot I'd expected to see at the obstacle course. "I think everybody was kind of nervous, though."

"Were there more colored kids in your class than white kids?"

"I think it's about even," I said. I started laughing. "You know what? I almost counted Darlene Jeffries with the white kids. I guess because I've known her forever. Besides, she's one of the coolest people I know."

Jackie closed her eyes and stood completely still for thirty seconds, and then she yelled, "Follow the Leader!" and started dancing the Pony like she'd lost her mind. Follow the Leader was her favorite game. So I started dancing, too, and then Jackie spun around three times and hopped on one foot down the hall toward my bedroom, and I hopped behind her. She turned at my bedroom door and did a pretend striptease as she went back down the hall toward the living room. She was shimmying her hips and shoulders and making motions like she was flinging clothes behind her as she went. I followed her, flapping my hands around because I was laughing too hard to do exactly what she was doing.

That's when she ran smack into my dad, who was walking out of the den. We both screamed and turned to run back to my bedroom.

I slammed the door shut behind us, and Jackie and I jumped on the closest bed.

"I will never be able to even *look* at your daddy again," Jackie said.

Then she had another attack and started kissing my Beatles poster.

"Stop it!" I said, trying to pull her away. "You can kiss Ringo, but don't you dare kiss George!"

Nobody ever laughed as much as we laughed that night.

CHAPTER 13

The next morning I grabbed a section of the newspaper as soon as Dad finished it. "I have to start collecting current events for my journal," I said.

"Well, don't cut anything out until your mother has had a shot at the paper, all right? I recommend Walter Cunningham's column."

To make Dad happy, I turned to the column. The title was BUSING IS NO BUST.

The first day of school desegregation in Windsor County began and ended without incident, and the critics of busing as a means of achieving racial balance in the schools were proven wrong. We are proud of the citizens of Windsor, city and county, who have provided an example for the rest of the country on how to achieve educational equality. Fact and reason won over rumor and hysteria. Now everyone should stand back and watch the children. They will lead the way. We have faith in these kids.

The best news? Less than 20 percent of school-age students failed to return to the public schools—and we predict that many of the 20 percent will return to the public schools within two years.

A glimmer of hope! Two years was a long time, but maybe it wouldn't take quite that long. Maybe next year, when we started seventh grade, Jackie's parents would let her come back. After all, she wouldn't be bused across town—we'd be going to West Windsor Junior High School, which is where we'd have gone anyway! I couldn't believe I hadn't thought of that before.

"Walter Cunningham is a genius!" I rattled the paper at Dad, like he did to us.

Dad looked over the top of the sports page. "Princeton man," he said.

Laura came in wearing a short-sleeved, hot pink dress with a white crocheted vest over it. She looked so cool. We walked down the driveway together.

"Hey, I like your outfit," I said.

"Hey, *merci beaucoup*. What's with the briefcase, Little Bit?"

I was carrying an old briefcase that Dad had thrown in the basement. It was big, brown, and shaped like the door of a doghouse—like an upside-down U. Inside, it still smelled like the basement. I had my books, math workbook, and pencils in it.

"It's amazing, but it's you," Laura said.

That made me feel good.

The second day of school was a little more normal, and except that it was still hard to remember everybody's name, it was pretty much like school had always been. I did miss Jackie, though. Sometimes I wanted to laugh at something and catch somebody's eye, but there wasn't any eye to catch. There was a boy named Kyle something on one side of me, and Henry Bailey behind me. I spent a lot of time staring out the window. There wasn't much to see out there, so I ended up wondering what Jackie was doing. It was kind of lonesome, except for recess and lunch, when I hung out with Amy Voorhees and a couple of the other girls. It felt weird to be so friendly with Amy all of a sudden. We'd known each other for ages and never been very close, but now it was like we were old pals. It was easier and quicker than having to make all new friends.

After lunch that second day, Miss Gohagan sat on the edge of her desk and opened a book. "I've decided that each day, after lunch, when you're too sleepy to work math problems, we are going to read a chapter from *The Adventures of Huckleberry Finn.* I'm going to read the first chapter today, and then we'll go around the room."

Well, that was all right. I didn't mind reading out loud, but I hoped we could do it from our desks and not have to go to the front of the room. That would be awful.

Miss Gohagan said, "Before I begin Chapter One, let me say that *Huckleberry Finn* was written by Mark Twain in 1886. He also wrote *The Adventures of Tom Sawyer,* and many other books and stories. *Huck Finn* has always been a controversial book, and an important book in American literature. You'll study it in more detail when you get to high school, and you'll learn then about some of the strong opinions people have about it.

"The book is about a white boy—Huckleberry—who runs away from his drunken father. He ends up running in the same direction as a runaway slave named Jim. Huck decides he'll help Jim escape down the Mississippi River to a state where slavery is banned, so he'll be free. As you'll see, they have all sorts of adventures on the way. They are always afraid that they might be caught and taken back to their old lives. As they face danger and trouble together, they become very, very close friends. Darlene, you and Victoria can visit later. Settle down, and listen as I read."

She stopped, and looked at us very seriously. "Now, I want to warn you," she said. "Bad things happen in the book. It's not a fairy tale. A lot of people die. . . ." Miss Gohagan looked at the book, and then she put it on her desk. "In fact, I think maybe it would be best if we didn't read this one."

But we were hooked, and she knew it. We wanted action, and blood, and fear—the kind of fear that made you shiver all over, and the shivering was fun because you knew it was in a book, and not real life.

"No, read it, Miss Gohagan!" David and Kyle said at the same time. We all laughed, and Miss Gohagan picked up the book and opened it to the first chapter.

Miss Gohagan must have wanted to be an actress before she decided to be a teacher, because she read the chapter with a lot of expression. After she read, we had science, and then math. We got math workbooks *and* a math book.

"Before we're dismissed," she said, "I have something important to discuss with you. Do you know what a clique is? A clique is a little circle of friends who stick together and don't let other people in the group. Now, I have noticed that some of you seem to be sticking together, maybe with people you've been friends with for a while. But from now on, when

I see the same people grouping together day after day, you can be sure that I'm going to break it up. From this day forward, cliques are banned in this classroom."

Miss Gohagan was young and pretty, but she was every bit as tough as Fierce Pierce.

Even though we had failed on the obstacle course, Miss Gohagan obviously hadn't given up on trying to help us come together as a team, because we spent our next recess organizing our class into a football team. On the way to the playground, I said hello to John Williams. I always thought of him as a friend, because in first grade he taught me how to snap my fingers.

"Hi, John," I said. "Remember this?" I snapped my fingers.

"Yeah," he said, and he snapped his back at me. He had long dark hair that hung over his ears and in his eyes. He looked cuter than he had in first grade.

"How do you like it here so far?" I asked.

John shrugged. "It's fine with me. I can get along anywhere, with anybody."

When we got to the playground, the boys were supposed to turn into a football team, and the girls had to be cheerleaders. Once we'd practiced a couple of times we were going to play the other sixth-grade classes.

But it was so hot that nobody wanted to run, or tackle, or even learn some real cheers from Darlene Jeffries, whose big sister was a tenth-grade cheerleader. The boys hung around for a while, and mostly they divided up between white boys and black boys and stood around in groups, until finally Henry Bailey walked over to Miss Gohagan. "Miss G.," he said, "it too *hot*."

Miss Gohagan sighed. "All right," she said. She fanned herself with the red booklet that she carried everywhere. "Maybe we can get Sporty to put up a volleyball net for us. Then we can pretend we're at the beach."

"I tell you what, Miss G.," Henry said as we walked back to the school, "tomorrow, maybe you could let us go back to that nice, shady obstacle course, and I can show you my plan for how we can all get over that Wall. I been working on how to do it."

"We'll give it another try sometime, Henry," Miss Gohagan said. "I think first we need to get to know each other a little better."

"I'm the Man with the Plan," Henry said.

At lunch, Kathy Harrell told me to sit next to her. In class she sat in the row next to mine, right beside Henry Bailey. She seemed to be pretty nice, and she had the kind of long straight blond hair that I'd always wanted. "It's okay for us to sit together," she said, "because we haven't sat together already. So Miss Gohagan can't accuse us of being a clique."

I put my tray down next to hers and opened my carton of milk. Kathy leaned toward me and whispered, "But what Miss Gohagan doesn't know is that we've got a *secret* clique. Watch this."

Kathy looked up and caught Carolyn Lohmann's eye. Carolyn was drinking milk through a straw, and without stopping she picked up her other hand and snapped her fingers one time.

Then Kathy looked at Amy Voorhees, and Amy snapped *her* fingers.

Kathy was laughing now. "See?" she said. "We're a *click*. Every time we pass each other in the hall, or in class, we just snap our fingers. It's like a secret code."

My milk tasted sour, and I thought I might get sick. What good was a secret code without Jackie to share it with? I finally said, "That's cool. Who's in it?"

"Just you, me, Carolyn, Amy, Holly Johnson, and Robin Sutton."

All the white girls in class. If Miss Gohagan figured out what was going on, she'd pitch a major fit. But if I didn't go along with it, maybe I wouldn't have any friends. Anyway, it was a funny idea—exactly the kind of thing Jackie would start herself. I sat there while Kathy told me a story about the time she went to summer camp for a week, and the clique she'd been in there, but I didn't hear much of what she said. I was too homesick for Jackie. If Jackie had come to EWE with me, I'd never have felt left out, even if she had been put in a different sixth-grade class. With Jackie around, I wouldn't be worried about joining a clique and getting in trouble.

But maybe we wouldn't get in trouble. The black girls were hanging out together a lot, too. Gaylyn and Darlene were talking a mile a minute, like they'd known each other forever. Desegregation had worked out great for them. I looked down the lunch table. All the girls were at one end, and the boys were at the other. Beastle sat on the edge of the girls' section. *She* would never get in trouble for being in a clique—she always seemed to be in a world of her own.

I watched her as we walked back to the classroom after lunch. Sure enough, she stayed off by herself. I sure didn't want to end up like *that*. I had to join the secret clique.

When I sat down at my desk after lunch, Miss Gohagan handed me a book. I had forgotten all about reading my chapter of *Huckleberry Finn*.

"You can sit at your desk to read, if you like, Amanda," she said. "Whatever makes you most comfortable."

So I opened the book to Chapter Two. I looked down at the first page and was taking a deep breath when I saw it.

The word *nigger* was right there in the first paragraph.

CHAPTER 14

I couldn't believe it. I turned a couple of pages like I was trying to find the right place to start. Miss Gohagan was sitting at her desk with her hands folded over her red booklet. She smiled. What was she trying to do to me? Maybe it was a test, so I started to read, but instead of saying the *n* word, I said "friend." The word was all through that chapter, and I had to make up new words as I went along. Sometimes I said "person," and sometimes I said "friend." It wasn't a very relaxing way to read out loud. Not only that, but I bet some of it didn't even make any sense.

I was *so happy* when I turned the page and saw the last sentence: "My new clothes was all greased up and clayey, and I was dog tired." But Huckleberry Finn couldn't have been more dog tired than I was when I finally sat down.

When the bell rang for us to go home at 2:45, I hung around to talk to Miss Gohagan. I waited beside her desk while she walked out the door. Her red booklet was on top of her desk, like always, and I looked at the first page. The title was *Making Desegregation Work: A Guide for Teachers in the Windsor County Schools.* Under that it said, *Phase I: Team Building.* I stepped back like I'd never been near her desk. A

74

guidebook for making desegregation work! Ha! This was all brand-new for her, too.

She walked back in and smiled. "I'm sorry, Amanda. Did you need to see me?"

"Yes. Miss Gohagan, did I do the right thing?" I asked. "Was that some kind of test?"

"What do you mean, Amanda?" she asked. She had the biggest blue-gray eyes, just like the eyes in my Madame Alexander doll—the one that's supposed to be Amy March from *Little Women*.

"Well, there was a word in my chapter that I'm not supposed to say," I told her. "You know, *n-i-g-g-e-r*." Even spelling it made me feel like a criminal, and before I did I made sure there wasn't anybody else around. From the minute I started talking, my mom had drilled it into me that I was never, ever, to use that word under any circumstances. (There were a couple of other words that were on the list, too, and it seemed like every year she added a new one.)

"No, it wasn't a test, Amanda," she said. "In fact, one of the reasons we're reading that book is so we can face issues like the use of that word and deal with them head on. I understand that you don't feel comfortable saying it, and that's good. But sometimes the only way to get rid of a problem is to tackle it and fight it. Do you understand?"

"I think so," I said, and I had to hurry to get to my bus. But I didn't understand at all. I didn't hate Miss Gohagan like Amy Voorhees had said she did, because putting everybody in alphabetical order was a normal, teachery thing to do. But this business about *Huckleberry Finn* was something else. I decided that Miss Gohagan not only had eyes like my Amy March doll, she also had exactly the same thing inside her head—nothing.

Miss Gohagan got somebody to put a volleyball net up for us, and we played the next day. It was okay, but I'm not very good at serving. Miss Gohagan had divided the teams up alphabetically, so I was on the same side as Henry Bailey and his sister. Every once in a while Henry would say something like, "That's yours, Beastle. Put it over the net, now."

And once when Kyle Gunderman was looking around for whose turn it was to serve, he said, "Oh, it's her turn," and pointed to Beastle.

"Hey, Beastle," Henry said. "It's your serve, woman. Get on back there, now. It's all right," he told Kyle. "You can call her Beastle."

Gaylyn Graves called out, *Mar-cell-uh!* Don't stand for his mess." But Beastle stood waiting to serve with a dreamy look on her face, like she was somewhere else. She didn't seem to hear either Henry or Gaylyn.

Since she didn't bother to complain about it, some of the boys kept calling her Beastle. They seemed to think it was funny, but I noticed they never said it when Miss Gohagan was close enough to hear them. Gaylyn and Victoria and the other black girls called her Marcella. Miss Gohagan called her Joy. I didn't know what to call her. In my mind, I always thought of her as Beastle, because that's what I called her when I told Jackie about school.

To get back to class, we walked beside a fence that separated the school from the street. There was an old black man walking by real slowly, and hot as it was he had on a brown suit and a brown hat with a black band around it. When Henry Bailey saw him, he acted like he'd gotten a jolt of electricity. "Hey!" he yelled. "Hey, Spaghetti Eddie! Spaghetti Eddie with the meatball eyes!"

The old man turned toward Henry and cussed, with his face all twisted. That made Henry laugh so hard that Miss Gohagan hurried up from the back of our line and told him to please keep it down.

It looked like Henry Bailey's favorite thing was calling people names. I was glad that he hadn't thought of one to call *me* yet.

Carolyn Lohmann was another one of Henry's victims. Carolyn was the biggest girl in our class. She wasn't quite as tall as Beastle, and she had red hair, breasts the size of a grown woman's, and a sort of an old-lady voice, high-pitched and quavery. For a while I wondered if she had that disease that makes you age really fast, but she was just way more developed than the rest of us. I had never seen anybody my age quite like Carolyn Lohmann.

Carolyn sweated so much that she had to bring a change of clothes to school for recess. Every day right before we went outside or to the gym, Miss Gohagan would let Carolyn go to the girls' bathroom down the hall and change. Carolyn kept her gym clothes in a brown paper bag on the shelf above the coat hooks at the back of our classroom. I would have died if it had been me.

Henry Bailey (who else?) was the one who started the teasing. First he called her "Sweaty Nettie," then he grabbed her bag off the shelf and said, "What is that *smell?*" He put his big face into the top of the bag and pretended to die. Then he tossed it to Joenathan, who threw it like a football toward Leonard Marvin. But Leonard wasn't looking, and John Williams caught the bag instead. He handed it to Carolyn and said in his slow, friendly way, "Now if mama was here she'd say, 'Y'all stop before you put somebody's eye out.' "

"Aw, what's the matter with you, man?" Henry asked. "We were just playing a little game of hot potato with Sweaty Nettie's dirty old clothes." He didn't act mad, though. It was hard to get mad at John Williams.

Carolyn shook the bag at Henry. "I bring in clean ones *every day,*" she said. But Henry laughed.

It was Henry Bailey's turn to read a chapter of *Huckleberry Finn,* and I was terrified of what might happen. I could feel the pages turn behind my back as he opened the book to Chapter Three. When he started reading, I started praying. I prayed that Henry Bailey wouldn't cause any trouble by reading that ugly word that I'd seen in the book the day before. I prayed that he would have the good sense not to start something, and then I did what Miss Elaine at Sunday school was always saying you shouldn't do—*I had doubts.* I doubted for a second there that even God could stop Henry Bailey from causing trouble if he took it into his head to start some, and then that made me think that all my prayers were useless. But he went on reading, and I don't know if he didn't have that word in his chapter or if he changed it when he got to it. All I know is he never said it. I couldn't tell you what he *did* say, but he didn't say that word, and that's all that mattered to me.

CHAPTER 15

The next day it rained, so we had to go to the gym and play basketball at recess. The last thing I wanted was for Henry Bailey to notice me. But he did.

Henry Bailey and the other boys on both teams were hogging the ball. They acted like there was no way a girl could dribble, much less shoot the ball. So all I did was run back and forth with the other girls, and when we got to the basket we stood and watched the boys throw the ball around and shoot. We were playing with twice as many people on each team as normal. We sounded like about ten teams, yelling, stomping, and smacking the ball. Plus every time Kathy, Carolyn, Amy, Holly, or Robin came by, we'd click at each other. Kathy was really good at clicking and making it look like it didn't mean anything. It felt great to be part of something again. It reminded me of the way I felt with Jackie.

Since it was a waste of energy, I finally stopped running back and forth, and I stayed near my own team's basket with my arms crossed, waiting for recess to end. But a wild throw on the other end sent the ball rolling to Beastle, who was on my team. She picked it up. Every boy on our team started screaming at her to throw it to him. But Beastle saw me standing near our basket and threw the ball to me. I dribbled it twice and made my layup. And since I'd never done it in front of these kids before, I jumped higher than I ever had before, made the shot, and came down feeling like, *So there, stupid boys.*

The boys stared with their mouths hanging open, but the game started right back up. They still believed *they* could play better than any girl who ever lived. Sports acted like a melting pot for the boys in our class. The black boys and the white boys always seemed to get along together fine when they were playing ball.

But Henry had lost interest in the game, and when I stayed behind at our basket again, he stayed with me. I knew he was still there, because I saw his big red Converse high-tops, and they didn't move. My mouth was dry, and when I finally looked up and tried to smile at him my lips stuck to my big billboard teeth.

"You can jump," he said finally.

"I've been working on that shot a long time."

We were almost trampled when the teams turned and came back to our basket, so I stepped out of bounds. After my great shot, I figured I might as well call it a day. Henry stepped out of bounds, too. He laced his fingers together and held his hands down in front of me with the palms up.

"You reckon you could jump even higher than that if I was to give you a boost?" he asked.

"I never tried it before, and anyway, it would be against the rules."

"I ain't talking about *basketball*," he said. He shook his

cupped hands in front of me. "Why don't you go down there, get a running start, and jump into my hands, and let's see how high you go."

I walked down the side of the court and turned to face him. "Come on," he said, shaking his hands again.

What if he was just trying to get me to do it so he could grab my ankle and make me fall?

"Come on, girl," he said again, so I started running, and as I got to Henry I stepped into his cupped hands and jumped up. It didn't go very well, but at least Henry hadn't done anything mean.

"That was awful," I said. "Let me try it again. I can go higher than that. But this time, just keep your hands steady. Don't try to throw me into the air. I think it'll work better if I just use your hands like a platform."

I got another running start, and this time Henry kept his hands perfectly still and flat, and when I jumped out of his palms I went a lot higher. I nearly fell when I landed, but Henry grabbed my arm and kept me up.

"We got it, now," he said. "See, this is the way it is. You and me will be the last two people, and you'll be giving a hand up to the small girls while I'm giving a hand up to the bigger kids who are left. And then it'll be just me and you, and we'll do our boost. See?"

I saw. I was going to be Henry's secret weapon for conquering the Wall.

"Now, what's your name?" Henry asked.

"Amanda Adams," I said. I guess I wasn't the only one having trouble keeping everybody straight.

"All right, Amanda Adams, I'm putting your name down in my notebook right now."

I figured that if Henry Bailey thought he needed me to get him over that Wall on the obstacle course, then he'd probably treat me like a person, and not call me names.

In fact, he didn't even call me "doofus" when I spilled french fries all over the cafeteria floor at lunch that day.

Sporty came over with a broom and dustpan.

"I'm really sorry," I said.

"Gotta tighten up there, Sporty," he said.

But the only thing Henry Bailey said was, "Amanda Adams, why did you throw your french fries on the floor?" And that made me laugh.

I set my tray down at the place next to Darlene Jeffries. Robin Sutton was across the table from us, and she snapped her fingers at me. "What time is it?" she asked, like she'd just snapped to get my attention.

"Lunchtime," I said, snapping my fingers back at her. Robin laughed.

When Amy walked behind my chair she clicked at me, and I clicked back. The way we acted, you would have thought that snapping your fingers was the funniest thing in the world.

But Darlene wasn't laughing, and suddenly I felt like a jerk. "What are you having for lunch, Darlene?" I asked, trying to include her in the conversation.

But Darlene wasn't buying. "Well, it ain't Rice Krispies, like you all are having," she said in her meanest way. "No snap, crackle, and pop over here."

Robin shrugged her shoulders. I didn't say anything else, but my feeling of power fizzled out. I liked Darlene. I had known her for years, a lot longer than I'd known Kathy and Robin and Carolyn.

Besides, if Darlene said anything to Miss Gohagan, I was going to get it.

It was Beastle's turn to read a chapter after lunch. She read clearly and carefully, and I was paying attention to the story this time. When she read the part where Huck says he didn't take no stock in mathematics, the whole class laughed. It seemed to me that I'd panicked for nothing, and that the n word wasn't going to be used anymore. But she was reading along, and she reached a line where she slowed way down, like maybe she'd lost her place, and then she read, "Miss Watson's servant, Jim, had a hair-ball as big as your fist. . . ." I knew she'd changed the word like I had. I looked at her again. Actually, she didn't look stupid at all.

I was the one who looked stupid the day Henry got me sent to the principal's office. He and I were at the end of our class line, walking down the hall to go to the library, when he started slowing down. I nearly stepped on him. "Walk faster, Henry," I said.

He stopped and laced his fingers together.

"Let's try our boost," he said. "Come on—Miss G. ain't looking. Come *on*."

I backed away from Henry, and then I ran toward him and planted my foot in his hands. I stretched up my hand to see if I could touch the ceiling. I couldn't even come close. As I came back down, I sailed right past the open doorway of Mr. Gordon's sixth-grade class. And about a hundred eyes were looking right at me.

"Run, fool!" Henry said. He grabbed my arm and we ran, but we couldn't help laughing the whole way.

We were still laughing when we turned the corner and piled up against Mr. Harrison, the principal.

We spent our whole library time sitting in the school office. There were four hard chairs lined up against the wall outside Mr. Harrison's door. Mrs. Leland sat at a desk in front of us, typing. Mr. Harrison had his door shut, but we could hear him talking on his phone. He had a loud voice. Henry lay across three of the chairs and tried to put his big feet in my lap. I scooted my chair over so he couldn't.

When our class left the library Miss Gohagan sent Kyle Gunderman and David Morgan to get us. Kyle and David both had on their blue Boy Scout uniforms. Usually Kyle didn't talk much to the black boys in our class. But from the minute David had walked in wearing that uniform, Kyle had been craning his neck to look at it. When they walked up to the office to get us, Kyle was asking David about his badges.

Henry shot up off the chairs when he saw them. "Miss Gohagan didn't have to send armed guards to come get us!" he said, so loud that Mr. Harrison came out to see what was going on.

"All right, now, Henry, keep your lips shut until you're back in your classroom," he said. Still, he couldn't help but smile when he saw Kyle and David. Then he looked down at me. "Amanda, no more running in the halls, right?"

"Right," I said.

Mrs. Leland had to put her two cents' worth in. "Amanda, remember to be careful who you follow. Some people will lead you straight into trouble, every time."

Henry's mouth fell open. "Dag! Now, how do you know she wasn't the one leading *me* into trouble?"

Mrs. Leland pulled a sheet of paper out of the typewriter. "I've known you since you were six years old," she said. She smiled, though, and gave Henry a little punch on the arm when he walked by her desk.

Kyle and David walked together down the hall, talking a mile a minute about Boy Scout stuff. I walked behind them, so Henry jumped in front of us and pretended he was leading a parade. He leaned backward and marched with his knees pumping high in the air, keeping time with an imaginary baton. I wanted to be mad at him for getting me in trouble, but he was so crazy, I had to laugh.

CHAPTER 16

For my first piano lesson with Mrs. Gandy, I had stuck my favorite recital piece in my briefcase. It was "My Grandfather's Clock." I liked it because it was fun to play, and it reminded me of the cabin at Sapphire Mountain. When we all sat around the fire outside and sang, it was one of our favorites.

When I got to Mrs. Gandy's classroom, the door was still closed. I peeked through the window in the door. Mrs. Gandy was talking to a black girl who was playing out of a beginner's music book. How much time could it take to play "Every Good Boy Does Fine"? I stood beside the door and hoped they wouldn't take too long. That hallway gave me the creeps.

When the door finally opened and the little girl came out, she looked at me like I was the one who'd kept *her* waiting. She was nothing but a fifth-grader. Sixth-graders, of course, were superior to fifth-graders.

"Come in, Amanda Adams," Mrs. Gandy said. Today she had two stools in front of the piano. "Come in and sit down here beside me. I'm sorry I kept you waiting, but today was Vanessa's first piano lesson, and we had a lot of material to

cover. Did you bring your piece to play for me? Good. Then you just get settled in, and whenever the spirit moves you, you just play. I'm going to sit way over here on the other side of this room, and you can pretend like I'm not even here."

I put my music on the piano and sat down on the stool. Mrs. Gandy rolled her stool over to the other side of the room and waited. I have a habit, before I start playing the piano, of running through the first several bars of the song in my mind, like I'm watching myself play. Then I start playing for real. Now my mind was almost blank. I took a deep breath and thought about campfires and singing off-key with Jackie. She loved this song, too.

When I finished, Mrs. Gandy rolled her stool back to the piano beside mine. "You know something?" she said. "I think you really like that song. That was done with *style*. But now I have a question. Was that your last recital piece?"

"Well, not the last one," I said. "It was the one before last."

"Um-hmm," Mrs. Gandy nodded. "You know how I know? That piece—why, you know it like the back of your hand, and I don't believe it provides a challenge to you, now does it?"

"No, I guess not," I said. "But I wanted to play something I felt, you know, comfortable with."

"Well, you played it just beautifully. But now we're going to get down to the nitty-gritty, and I'm going to help you play it even better. You want to know how?"

"Sure," I said, shrugging.

"Well, first, you're using too much of that stool. You sit on it like you're sitting there waiting for a bus." Mrs. Gandy shifted her weight so that she was sitting on her whole stool and not just on the front half of it. She played a boring little scale. "See, honey? You can't really reach the keys like that. Now move forward a little more, and you give yourself some room to swing from side to side and really get down." Mrs. Gandy moved to the front of her stool, and played a few bars of something fast and happy.

I had to grin at her. The way Mrs. Gandy could make the piano sound made me feel like that night at the outdoor concert, when the "Little Fugue" was rising up in the night. Mrs. Gandy smiled back at me, threw her head back, and laughed as she ended her song with a dramatic flourish.

"Do you think I'll ever be able to play like that?" I asked.

"Child, I hope you're going to play a whole lot better," Mrs. Gandy said. She straightened up the pages of "My Grandfather's Clock." "Let's try it out, now. You sit like I told you, and let's make that old clock really tick!"

At first it was hard to play the notes and remember to sit forward and move like Mrs. Gandy did. But whenever I forgot, Mrs. Gandy put her hands on my shoulders, and said in my ear: *Move* with it, sugar, move with it!"

"I've never been taught piano like this before," I said. "I made a whole lot more mistakes when I tried to move with it."

"That's all right, little girl, that's all right. Now, I'm going to give you this book of music to try out. It could be that it's a little more advanced than you're used to, but we'll just have to figure this out as we go. I want you to pick out one song—it doesn't matter which one—and play it for me next week."

I took the book and flipped through it. Some of the songs did look like they might be hard, but maybe if I couldn't play these songs very well, Mrs. Gandy would move me down to an easier book. Then I stopped. "Oh," I said.

"What is it, sugar?" Mrs. Gandy asked. She looked at the book. " 'Jesu, Joy of Man's Desiring,' " she said, and she started playing the beginning of it. "Do you like that song, Amanda?"

"I love it," I told her. "But I can't believe there's a song by *Bach* in here. I'm afraid this is way above my level."

"Shoot, you'll be playing this in no time," Mrs. Gandy said. "And when you practice, I want you to practice with your arms, your shoulders, and your tailbone, too. I'll see you next Monday, Amanda."

I walked out and headed down the hall. Some black boys were hanging around the doorway of Sporty's office, and when they saw me coming they started acting funny, like something secret was going on in there. I held my breath and walked on past them, and they stared me down the whole time. A couple of them were boys from my class. Henry Bailey was there, and he acted like he was trying to block the doorway so I couldn't see inside. It felt like it took a week to walk past them, and my heart was beating like I'd been running for miles. It felt like there really was a Beastle in the hallway—not Henry's sister, but a nightmare Beastle with cold, filthy breath.

* * *

"They're probably planning a way to burn the school down," Jackie said when I told her about the strange way the boys had acted. She and I were practicing roundoffs in my backyard. A roundoff started out just like a cartwheel, but in the middle of it you had to remind your feet to come down at exactly the same time, side by side. My brain was having trouble with that, but Jackie had finally trained herself to do it every time.

"Why would they burn their own school down?" I asked. "That doesn't make much sense."

She turned a perfect cartwheel and said, "I meant to do a cartwheel that time." Then she did a roundoff. It wasn't as perfect as her cartwheel, but you could tell what it was.

I tried another roundoff, and this one was almost right. "You just need to remember to put your feet together while they're still in the air," Jackie said. "You've almost got it. They'd rather see the school burnt to the ground than have a bunch of white kids in it."

"I don't think so," I said. "Maybe they're just smoking cigarettes."

"I know—they're the Clique Patrol!" Jackie said. "They've found out about your secret clique."

I fell right in the middle of my cartwheel. "Very funny," I said. I had gotten the nerve up to talk to Kathy Harrell. I'd said, "I love the clique, Kathy, but if we keep it up, Miss Gohagan is going to find out."

Kathy had said, "Yeah, I guess you're right." But I still heard fingers snapping every once in a while.

"Are there any cliques in your new school?" I asked Jackie. What if she was in a clique without me?

"Just the bathroom cliques," Jackie said. "We have to go to the bathroom in shifts because there are only four *small* toilets in the whole church—two for girls, and two for boys. So girls with last names beginning with *A* through *E* go at the same time. We're the Toilet Bowl Clique! But it won't be long before we get a brand-new building. We're already too big for the church building, so they're going to build a separate school. Our room is *so small* you wouldn't believe it. But Larry Bernard is in my class." We had both had a crush on Larry since third grade. He was gorgeous, and now he was all Jackie's.

"Do you like going to that school?" I asked. I wasn't sure what I wanted to hear.

"Of course! See, since we're small and private and everything, we get to do a lot of special stuff. We take lots of field trips, and do neat crafts and activities. We're going to learn everything about the space program, and during the Easter holiday we're going to get to go to Florida and see NASA. Besides, since the classes are small, we get more individual attention. I'll probably be ready for college a year early."

My head was spinning. Jackie had never been the type to want individual attention from a *teacher*. I thought hard, looking for something I could tell her about my new school, something that would make her jealous.

"Well, while you're in college, I'll already be a famous author. I'm starting to write a book right now, called *The Beastle*. It will be a horror book, and they'll make it into the scariest movie of all time. The whole thing will take place in the basement of EWE." Jackie was laughing, which made me try to think of even funnier things to say. "There will only be three characters: Beastle, John Williams, the only boy brave enough to face Beastle, and Mrs. Gandy, the music teacher." I stopped there, because it didn't feel right, making fun of Mrs. Gandy. I liked her better than I liked Miss Gohagan.

"Yeah!" Jackie said. "Mrs. Gandy, the music teacher, who's too fat to get out of the basement!"

"She's not fat."

"You said she was big. You told me that after your orientation. She's too fat to get out of the basement."

"But the main character is Beastle," I said, trying to change the subject. "She stays down in that basement, and the other kids go to the bottom of the stairs and yell down the basement hall, trying to get her to come out of the dark. Then one day I guess she just goes nuts. She sneaks onto a school bus and rides into the west side of town."

"No, no! Don't let her come *here*!" Jackie yelled.

"Yes, that's right. She gets into New Canaan Academy, and the National Guard comes and shoots tear gas at her. They don't mean to hurt her, they just want to stun her so they can carry her out and lock her up. But it turns out that Beastle doesn't cry tears, she cries blood, and she cries so much from the tear gas that she bleeds to death. The end."

Jackie couldn't stop laughing. "That's the craziest thing I ever heard. It would be creepy, though. Okay, Follow the Leader! Do six roundoffs in a row, then five cartwheels."

It felt good to turn upside down and pretend that my feet were walking on the sky. I could pretend that everything was reversed—that I was still in school with Jackie and nothing had changed.

CHAPTER 17

Once a week Miss Gohagan put us into different groups to work on our journals, which forced us to get to know each other. So far my journal had two news articles in it and one interview. The way it worked, two people interviewed each other at the same time. Miss Gohagan had given us a mimeographed sheet of twelve questions, and the interview had to cover at least six of them. You could make up your own questions, too, as long as they weren't silly.

My first interview was with Henry's sister. At the top of a page in my notebook I wrote, "Interview with Marcella Bailey."

"I want to be called Joy," she said. She was watching me write. "See, I've been called Marcella since first grade," she said. "And I've been going to school with Gaylyn and Victoria and some of these other ones all these years. They can't remember that now I want to go by my middle name, and so none of the new people ever call me by it, either. All I get is 'Marcella.' "

"There's nothing *wrong* with the name Marcella," I said. I didn't say so, but it was pretty obvious that it was better than being called Beastle. I didn't think of her as Beastle anymore—not since I'd told Jackie about the nightmare Beastle. Now I mostly thought of her as Henry's sister. I erased "Marcella" and wrote in "Joy."

I picked questions that had short answers, so I found out that her birthday was June 12, her favorite color was yellow, and her favorite season was spring. She liked to read and roller-skate, but she didn't have any real hobbies, like collecting stamps or coins. She had one brother (Henry) and one younger sister. They lived in Smoketown, which was what people called the neighborhood around Galt Brothers Tobacco. Her favorite food was spaghetti.

If Miss Gohagan thought this was a good way to make new friends, she was crazy. It wasn't natural to find out about people by asking them questions, like it was a job interview or something.

Anyway, the interview didn't make me like her any better. Even if I didn't think of her as Beastle, I had no respect for anybody with so little gumption. She let her own brother call her names and didn't fight back! I wasn't much of a fighter, either, but I sure wouldn't let my *family* get away with stuff like that.

Then it was her turn to interview me. She kept her head down, looking at the sheet of questions and then writing the answers in her notebook, so I mostly just stared at the part in her hair. I got kind of hypnotized looking at it, and I didn't stop to think about how some of my answers were going to sound.

"What's your favorite color?"

"Green."

"What's your favorite food?"

"Pizza."

"If you could be anything in the world, what would you like to be?"

"A conductor."

It came out before I even had time to think about it. I'd never even mentioned wanting to be a conductor to Jackie.

She looked up at me. "Really?" she said. "Like a music conductor?"

"Yes, like Toscanini," I said. "He conducted orchestras all over the world."

"Tos-ca-ni-ni," she said. "How do you spell that?"

I had found out about Toscanini and conducting in a book from the school library.

At first I didn't like the library at EWE. It wasn't nearly as cheerful as the library at West Windsor. It was full of dark wood shelves and tables. After a while, though, I started to like the spookiness, because it made choosing a book more exciting. There was a strange collection of books in it, too. Sometimes it seemed like they'd gotten adult books mixed up with the kids' books. When I found a book called *How to Conduct a Small Orchestra,* I nearly jumped. It was a thin book with a dark green cover. The title was on the spine and on the front in gold letters. It was old, with the name of a different library stamped on it. I held the book for a while, not even wanting to look inside yet. If I could learn to conduct a small orchestra, I would be way ahead of Jackie and her private-school friends. Then it wouldn't matter at all if they graduated a year early. Maybe I really would be famous—the youngest conductor in history!

Miss Gohagan clapped her hands to get everyone's attention. "Finish up, and form your discussion groups," she said. "Each person in the group should tell about one news article read during the past week."

I was in a group with Henry and his sister, Kyle Gunderman, Kathy Harrell, and Darlene Jeffries.

We dragged our desks into a little group, and then we all sat there and looked at each other.

Miss Gohagan came over to help us along. "Darlene, why don't you get the ball rolling," she said. She moved on to the next group, and we just sat there again.

"I read an article about fashions," Darlene said finally.

"Girl, you can't be talking about fashions," Henry said. "You supposed to be talking about a current event."

"Miss Gohagan told me that I could," Darlene said. "And don't you interrupt me again." Sometimes she sounded like the kind of adult who isn't interested in talking to kids. "Boots are supposed to be even bigger this fall than they were last year," she said. She held up an article from the Sunday paper that showed a model wearing lace-up boots with a long skirt. "But will my mama buy me a pair? No."

Kyle Gunderman's desk faced the windows. He suddenly said, "Gross. I think somebody hocked a lugie on our window."

"Hocked a *what?*" Henry Bailey said, and we all turned to see what Kyle was talking about.

"A lugie," Kyle said. "You know, a wad of spit."

"I ain't never heard it called a lugie before," Henry said. "And where'd you get that word *hock*? That's a new one on me, too."

"It means spit," Kyle said. "*You* know. Don't tell me you never heard *that* before! And anyway, look right there, right in the middle of the middle window. What does that look like to you?"

Henry got up and looked, and came back to say it was one of those thick little webs, like worms sometimes build in trees. "Anyway," Henry said, "*hock* sure don't mean nothing about spitting. Hock's what you do at the pawnshop, when you take something in, and they give you money for it."

"Oh, yeah, that's right," Kyle said, "but it can mean spit, too."

"I never heard the word *hock* at all," Kathy said.

"These boys is making up words," Darlene said in a bored tone of voice. But we weren't bored. This was just the kind of group discussion we all liked. I wished that Jackie were there. Then I thought about Jackie writing her composition using the dictionary.

"Get the dictionary!" I told Kyle. "We'll see what it says."

Miss Gohagan smiled at us as Kyle brought the big dictionary from the back of the classroom to our group. He flipped through it, looking for the letter *H*.

"*Hock* is in here!" Kyle said excitedly. He laughed so loudly that Miss Gohagan looked over from the group she was helping. "Look what it says!" he said, trying to hold his voice down.

I looked across at the page to where Kyle was pointing his

finger. There, in double brackets, it said, "with loss of nasal as in *soft, tooth.*"

"With loss of nasal!" Kyle said.

"That's got to do with how you say it, I think," I said. But I snorted back a laugh.

"Okay, okay, okay," Kyle said, holding his hand out in front of him like he was trying to stop me. "Let's just think about something unfunny. Somebody say something unfunny."

"Dead puppies," Henry said, with a completely blank expression on his face.

That did it. We all laughed like idiots, until Miss Gohagan assigned us five math problems to solve as a punishment. We had to stay in the classroom and work while the rest of the class went to the library. As soon as Miss Gohagan left the room to walk the rest of the class down the hall, Kyle Gunderman leaned over to my desk and said in a loud whisper, "Dead puppies!"

All of us laughed again, but Darlene said, "We're going to be working math problems from now on if you all don't hush."

We laughed real softly, like a bunch of spies sharing a quick joke before we jumped out of the airplane and landed in enemy territory. (Jackie always did say I pretended too much.) It felt good to joke around, and I decided to impress Darlene and Kathy.

"Last year, a friend of mine got in trouble with the dictionary, too," I said. I was talking louder than normal. "Remember, Darlene, when we were supposed to write two hundred words about a book we'd read? Jackie just listed the first two hundred words in the dictionary! She got in front of the whole class and started reading words like they were a poem or something, but when she got to *abate*, our teacher, Fierce Pierce, made her sit down and gave her a D."

I had tried to make it sound interesting and funny. But Kyle was still working math problems, and Henry was looking at me like he was waiting for me to finish the story. Kathy kind of laughed, in a polite way. Darlene shook her head. "Jackie Charles," she said. "Where is that girl this year?"

"She went to another school," I said. I certainly didn't want to get into *that* with Darlene. I bent over my paper to hide my red face.

It was a relief when Miss Gohagan came in and checked our work and sent us down to the library. I didn't even look at the books. I went and sat on a step stool in a corner of the nonfiction section where the bookshelves threw long, dark shadows. All I could think about was how Jackie was happy making new friends at her new school and starting new jokes that I didn't know anything about, while I was stuck here in this place where nobody had a sense of humor at all.

I started moving the books around on the shelves, so that they were out of order. It made me feel better to know that the next person looking for one of those books would have a terrible time finding it.

I stood up when I heard someone coming down the aisle on the other side of the shelves. It was Henry's sister. She walked along slowly, running one finger along the backs of the books and humming so softly I could barely hear it. I peeked through the gap over the tops of the books in front of me. She must have heard me move, because she stopped and looked through the gap on her side. She smiled at me.

"Wrote a whole paper using words out of the dictionary?" she said. "I bet that did sound like a funny poem." She started humming again and walked on.

CHAPTER 18

"I don't want to hear that foot tapping on that pedal," Mrs. Gandy said. "Keep your heel on the ground, keep the sole of your foot on the pedal, and quit that tapping."

I hadn't played even half of my new song before Mrs. Gandy stopped me. I had picked a song in the new book that didn't have any sharps or flats at all, and I thought I was doing pretty good.

"Maybe I ought to take my shoes off," I said.

"Maybe you ought to do like I say. Now, what you do is, you play your chord, and *then* you use the pedal to sustain the sound. Listen while I do it. Hear that? Don't start pushing the pedal as soon as you start your chord, or the pedal's gonna pick up your last beat. Little girl, who taught you to pedal? This is not one of those paddleboats—you're not going to paddle this piano down the hall and out of this school. Never mind, we'll get her right yet."

Somehow I didn't mind when Mrs. Gandy criticized my playing. She always did it in a way that made me laugh, but she made me want to try harder to get my songs right.

"Who taught you how to play the piano, Mrs. Gandy?" I asked her.

Mrs. Gandy shook her head. "The meanest little old lady in Sandy Fork, North Carolina," she said. "Sandy Fork, if you don't know it, is down near the coast, and that's where I grew up. Now, when I say it was near the coast, I mean it. We used to walk down the side of the road and pick up pieces of rock with fossilized seashells in them. I'll bring one in to show you sometime. Anyway, my family belonged to the Sandy Fork A.M.E. Church. It was a teeny-tiny little old church with a front door painted lavender and a matching lavender birdhouse set up on a post out back. Miss Nancy Plum was the church organist, and when I was ten years old and she was probably close to seventy, she decided that if she didn't train somebody else to play the piano in church, why, she might pass away and then where would we be? So she taught me to play in pain and suffering. She whacked my knuckles with a pencil every time I played a wrong note."

"Did she teach you how to play the organ, too?"

"No, child, Miss Plum wouldn't let *anybody* touch that organ. I believe she would have been satisfied to die knowing that it would never be touched again. But I loved the piano in spite of Miss Plum, and I determined that I was going to go to college and learn to be a music teacher, so that children wouldn't have to learn in such a hard way. I'm thankful she taught me, though, I truly am. Now let's try that last song one more time, and let me see you *move*."

When I left Mrs. Gandy's room that day, there were a couple of boys in Sporty's doorway. If I could get behind them without them hearing me, maybe I'd find out what was going on. I walked as quietly as I could, and they never heard me coming.

* * *

"So, what *was* going on?" Jackie asked. I hadn't seen her as much lately. The Saturday before, the New Canaan Academy had held a bake sale and barbecue to raise money for supplies and equipment. I had spent a lot of time in the Secret Garden that day. New Canaan Christian Church was too far away for me to be able to hear anything that might be going on there, but while I sat on a piece of wood and tried to imagine that I was safe and invisible behind high walls, I could almost hear people laughing and having a big time at the barbecue.

Now we were getting caught up while we spent the morning building a raft out of tree limbs and twine. When it was finished we carried it through the woods behind Jackie's house, to a little creek that ran back there. The creek wasn't deep enough for the raft to float, but we put the raft in the widest part and the water flowing past it made it seem almost real.

"I *think* Sporty was singing and playing a guitar. But when I got to the door, the boys saw me. Then whatever was going on stopped. They acted like it was top secret."

I stepped carefully onto the raft. "Aaah—I think it's going to hold. Now, you be Jim, and I'll be Huck. We're on the lookout for Pap, because I'm afraid he's coming after me to kill me." I had told Jackie most of the story that I knew so far, but I hadn't mentioned that Jim was a slave, or that he was a black. I just said that Huck and Jim were on a raft going down the Mississippi River and were having adventures as they went. If I had told her *everything,* I figured she wouldn't play the part of Jim.

104

Because no matter what she said, I still thought she was probably prejudiced. If she weren't, wouldn't she have talked her mom and dad into letting her go to school with me? Sometimes I wondered about myself, too. I hadn't wanted to go to the black school. Some nights after my bath I looked at my face in the bathroom mirror and tried to figure out what I really looked like. Laura told me that the reflection you see in the mirror isn't what everybody else sees, because it's reversed. That's why if you hold a book up to a mirror, the writing is all backward. I wondered if seeing myself backward meant that I couldn't see the signs of prejudice on my face, and everybody else could. But if that were true, shouldn't I be able to read the prejudice on Jackie's face, since I saw her unbackward? I could sure see the prejudice on the faces of the people in that newspaper picture of the black girl trying to walk to school. Jackie didn't look like that. Maybe it was her parents who were prejudiced, and they were rubbing off on her. Maybe she'd grow out of it.

I looked at Jackie. She sat on one end of the raft with her knees pulled up under her chin. "They must be doing something illegal," she said. "Don't you think? The whole school's probably running some kind of drug ring, or something. Maybe the reason they're singing and stuff is because they're all high on marijuana."

"For somebody who hates to pretend things, you sure do have a crazy imagination," I said.

"Well, we really *are* getting too old to play pretend stuff. Let's go play a real game—Aggravation, or Operation, or something."

To Jackie the important part had been the building and

the launching. After all our hard work, I hated to leave the raft in the creek.

"We could play *Gilligan's Island,*" I said. Sometimes we pretended like the creek was the lagoon. The raft could be the wreck of the *Minnow.*

But Jackie said, "Tell me more about the hideous Beastle."

I tried to think of something good. "Beastle's favorite color is yellow. The whites of her eyes are yellow, so everything she sees looks like a different shade of yellow."

"Ewwww!" Jackie said. Then she jumped up and yelled, "Follow the Leader!" She ran through the woods, zigzagging from side to side to make it harder. I zigzagged behind her, and we went to her room and talked until my mom picked me up.

Jackie would have been jealous if she had known that I got to interview John Williams. I sat in the desk beside his. John slid down in his chair and stretched his legs way out. He was completely relaxed. I was a nervous wreck.

I kept reminding myself of Mom's advice on how to handle social situations. "Don't think too much about yourself," she said. "Try to think about how you can make the other person comfortable."

Once I started asking him questions, it went a little better. I loved knowing his favorite food (cheeseburgers), his favorite season (winter, because he went snow skiing over Christmas vacation), and other personal facts that I could pull out when Jackie went on and on about New Canaan Academy.

John almost ruined it when we finished the interview and he said, "Hey, whatever happened to your friend, Jackie? Did she move, or something?"

"No, she's going to private school this year," I said in a low voice.

"Man, she copped out, huh?" he said. He pushed his hair out of his eyes.

"Yeah," I said. I pushed my hair out of my eyes, too. Miss Cool.

As we kept reading one chapter a day from *Huckleberry Finn,* everybody seemed to know the secret about not using the *n* word. Sometimes you could tell that people were stumbling around to come up with something different. Most of them settled on *slave.*

But then it was Scott Monroe's turn to read Chapter Fifteen. I guess he just wasn't thinking. Anyway, at the very end of the chapter, he read the word.

I felt my stomach heave. He looked kind of surprised as soon as he'd said it, but then he finished the chapter, and I started breathing again.

Miss Gohagan perked up, and as Scott took the book back to her she said, "Does anyone have any comment to make about what Scott read today?" Nobody said anything. That didn't stop her, though. "Huck uses a word for *Negro* that is very hurtful, doesn't he? He is so used to the old way of treating black people like property that even though he is beginning to change his attitude toward Jim, he still carries a lot of prejudice around, doesn't he? But Huck is getting better in his attitude, don't you think? Don't you think that the fact that Huck feels bad for hurting Jim's feelings is a big step forward? In Chapter Fifteen he finds it hard to apologize to him, but he *does* apologize. He's making real progress!"

But progress was *not* being made in our class. We were on the playground the next morning playing kickball when some of the black boys surrounded Scott.

"You just loved saying that word, didn't you?" Leonard Marvin asked. Henry Bailey and Leonard were standing side by side, facing Scott like they were a firing squad or something. We were all on the same team, and our team was up. Carolyn Lohmann had just kicked the ball over Amy Voorhees's head, and she was steaming toward first base, sweating up a storm.

"Hey, it wuddn't me that wrote it," Scott said. "Beat up Mark Twain."

Leonard didn't have an answer for that, so Henry said, "It wuddn't no Mark Twain said it in Miss Gohagan's class yesterday, now was it?" He moved closer to Scott and said something to him that I couldn't hear.

"What did you say?" Scott asked, and his face was red.

"I don't chew my cabbage twice," Henry said. That was his way of saying he wasn't going to repeat what he'd said. He spat on the ground.

David Morgan came over.

"Y'all stop acting like that," he said. "You knew that word was in that book, Henry. It doesn't mean a thing to us."

Henry opened his mouth, and that's when I stepped forward. "Come on, Henry," I said. I couldn't believe I was getting in the middle of this. I tried to keep my voice casual. "Let's practice our boost."

Henry turned and glared at me, and the Twenty-third Psalm started playing in my head. ("Yea, though I walk through the valley of the shadow of death. . . .") I braced myself.

But Henry turned his back on Scott and laced his fingers together. "All right, Amanda Adams," he said. "Let's try to go for some *real* height this time."

I went back to the fence around the playground and turned to face Henry. Before I ran, I reached behind me and curled my fingers around the links. I pushed off from the fence like an Apollo rocket, running toward Henry's open hands.

Nothing else happened that day, but I had a feeling that the problems weren't over.

CHAPTER 19

Miss Gohagan had asked us to prepare oral reports on any topic, and I decided my topic would be how to conduct a small orchestra.

I talked about how the conductor has to know the music for all the different instruments in the orchestra, and that he uses his hands, eyes, and whole face to tell them how it should be played. I showed how a conductor uses the right hand to beat the time, and the left hand to tell the orchestra to play softer (hand goes down) or louder (hand goes up).

"It's harder than it sounds," I said. "It's like patting your head and rubbing your stomach at the same time."

I sat down and tried to cool off. I get too worked up when I have to stand in front of the class and talk.

Henry Bailey got up after I was done and walked to the front of the room. He stood with his arms crossed and said, "The subject of my oral report is 'White People.' "

Nobody said anything, and Miss Gohagan just looked up from her grade book, then nodded at him to go on.

"White people all look alike," Henry said. He didn't use any notes. He acted like he'd been thinking about this a long time. "They have little pinched-in noses, skinny little lips, and lank old hair like weeds."

That sounded just like my hair.

"Sometimes I think that when God decided to make white people, that's when ugly was invented," Henry continued. "And white people have a funny smell, too. I can't describe it just exactly, but it kind of reminds me of the way a chicken smells after it's been sitting out in the rain."

Henry looked at Miss Gohagan like he was daring her to say anything; then he walked back to his desk and sat down. Nobody made a noise.

Miss Gohagan made a note in her grade book and looked up. "Let's discuss."

Nobody moved.

Miss Gohagan stood up. "What color am I? Am I the same color as Amy Voorhees?"

I nodded, along with everybody else.

"Am I?" Miss Gohagan asked. "Look closely. I have a very light complexion, but Amy has more olive skin tones. Look at Eddie and David. Are they the same color?"

Well, you could see that David was more of a tan color and Eddie was dark brown.

"What if I divided this class up by color?" Miss Gohagan said. "No two of you are exactly the same shade. We'd end up divided into twenty-eight separate pieces, wouldn't we? Darlene, you wouldn't be able to talk to Gaylyn, and Henry wouldn't be able to look over Amanda's shoulder every day to see what page of our science book he's supposed to be on.

"What I want you to learn this year—even if you don't learn anything else—is that *we need each other*, just like Huck Finn and Jim need each other. We can waste our time trying to divide up by skin tone, or we can accept the fact that each of us is different on the outside, and learn about each other on the inside, where it really matters. Leonard, what is the problem?"

Leonard Marvin had turned around in his seat to face Scott Monroe, who sat right behind him. "I heard you," Leonard was saying. "I'd just as soon knock you upside your head as look at you."

Miss Gohagan walked over to Leonard. His was the first desk in his row. She said quietly, "What is going on here, Leonard?"

Leonard turned around and scowled at her. He jerked his thumb over his shoulder toward Scott. "He's making comments I don't appreciate," he said.

I turned to look out the window. I didn't want to hear or see anything else, but then it was so quiet that I turned back.

Scott had his head down, staring at the top of his desk. "Scott?" Miss Gohagan said. "Let's get this out in the open, please."

Scott looked up at her. "Why is it all right for Henry to say that kind of stuff about white people, but if I said anything like that about colored people, I'd probably be expelled or something? I'm sick of it, that's all."

"Nobody asked you to come to this school, anyway," Leonard said, and Henry of course had to jump in there with, "That's right. Ain't nobody asked you to come to this school."

"No, they just *made* me," Scott said.

I cut my eyes to the right to look at Kyle Gunderman. I had a feeling that he felt sort of the same way Scott did.

When I had interviewed him for my journal, Kyle had told me that he had been chosen to be a hall monitor at his old school for this year, but then desegregation had come along. "And when we got here," he said, "they already had their hall monitors picked." I didn't write any of that down, because it didn't answer the question I'd asked, which was, "What is one thing you like about school?"

Miss Gohagan walked back toward my side of the room. "Henry, I have a question for you," she said. "Who was your report about?"

The back of my neck shivered as Henry breathed behind me.

"White people," he said.

"Who, exactly?" Miss Gohagan asked. "Can you tell us the names of the people you were thinking of when you wrote your report? Was Scott one of the people you meant?"

I held my breath. "I wasn't thinking of nobody in particular," Henry said. One of his feet kicked the leg of my desk. "I didn't have nobody in mind."

Miss Gohagan nodded. "Nobody in particular. You were talking about a group, in general?"

"That's right."

"That's what I thought," Miss Gohagan said. "Because it sounded like the kind of speech you might hear from a member of the Ku Klux Klan. They aren't talking about specific blacks when they make their hate speeches. They're talking about a group of people without faces or names. I expect Henry has heard parts of such speeches before, and the oral report he gave was very much like them."

She stopped and looked around the room. "I don't ever want to hear this kind of hate talk from my students again. Not in this classroom, and not outside this classroom."

She stopped again, and when she started talking again her voice was calmer. "Haven't you learned this year that once you get to know people who are different from you, everything changes? Suddenly John Williams isn't just a white boy, he's a kid whose hair keeps falling in his eyes who can draw Spider-Man like a professional. And Beatrice Young isn't just a black girl, she's an honorary member of the high-school drama club. Beatrice has performed in the high school's annual class play ever since she was in third grade."

I was amazed to see Kyle raise his hand. "Miss Gohagan?" he said. "Since you're talking about talents that people have, you ought to say that Blake can bark like a dog. And he can do this weird thing with his eyes."

That made everybody laugh. Blake Murray was a white boy who could bark better than Lassie, and he could whine like Lassie, too. His other trick was that he could make his eyeballs roll all the way up in his head so you couldn't see anything but whites. It was spooky.

Miss Gohagan shook her head as Blake let his eyeballs roll back down where they belonged. "I'm sure that many of you have talents I can only imagine," she laughed. "Now, get out your math workbooks and turn to page twenty-seven."

Miss Gohagan's red booklet must have had a section that said, in big print: IF NOTHING ELSE WORKS, HAVE THE CLASS DO A FEW MATH PROBLEMS. She was an awfully new teacher. Probably in a few more years she wouldn't need a red booklet to tell her what to do. I wished I had a red booklet with all the answers.

When the final bell rang, Miss Gohagan said, "Henry, spare me a minute of your time, please."

I wished I could stay and maybe hear what Miss Gohagan had to say, but it was piano lesson day. As I walked toward the stairs to go down to the basement, I saw a group of black boys from my class hanging out at the top of the steps. David Morgan, Eddie Taylor, and Bobby Nance were there, and I think Leonard Marvin. They were all grouped around Blake Murray. I got a cold feeling in my stomach, and I turned to see if there were any teachers close by. There weren't.

Then I heard Bobby Nance say, "Dag! Do that again, man!"

They were watching Blake roll his eyes up in his head.

CHAPTER 20

When I got to Mrs. Gandy's room, Vanessa was still in there. Her lesson ran late a lot. I sighed and sat down on the floor beside Mrs. Gandy's door. It wasn't fair. I wondered if Mrs. Gandy liked Vanessa better than she liked me. She probably did, since Vanessa was black. That was *really* not fair, but I could see that Mrs. Gandy might prefer to teach black children how to play the piano.

I leaned my head back against the wall and felt like the smallest person in the world. There was nothing but long, dark hallway stretching down to the stairwell, and there wasn't even any light coming out of Sporty's office because his door was closed. I thought that maybe this was how Neil Armstrong felt right after he got over the fun of jumping around on the moon. Even though the lunar module was right there and old Buzz Aldrin was in it waiting for Neil, he probably had a minute or two where he wondered how he had gotten to be so far from home. Then I had another thought: What if Neil Armstrong had wanted somebody *else* to go on *Apollo 11* with him, but they'd let Buzz Aldrin go instead? What if the worst part was, when he walked back into the lunar module, instead of seeing a good friend, it was somebody he hardly even knew?

Jackie, I thought, with my eyes closed, where are you?

After Henry's oral report, we had ended up laughing at Kyle. But it didn't feel like everything was fine. It was like there had been an earthquake, and once it was over we all stood around, scared to move because we were afraid the ground would start shaking again. I imagined that when the ground finally split open, the nightmare Beastle would roar up out of it.

"You sleeping?"

I opened my eyes. Vanessa stood there staring down at me. She said, "You better wake up and go on in there. Mrs. Gandy's waiting for you."

I couldn't stand to look at Vanessa's round little face, with her big dark eyes staring at me and her two little-girl ponytails sticking out over each of her ears. I gave her a mean look. It wasn't much. Jackie was the one who was really good at putting other people down.

Mrs. Gandy could tell I was grumpy. "What's on your mind, Amanda?" she asked.

"I hate everything," I said. I didn't want to tell her that I hated Vanessa for keeping me waiting, and that I hated going to a school where black kids and white kids kept getting on each other's nerves. I wanted life to be peaceful, with a little fun thrown in.

Mrs. Gandy kept looking at me, to see if I wanted to say anything more.

"I wish," I told her, "that people could be in harmony, you know, so life could be like music. Like the 'Little Fugue.'" I sat on my piano stool, and Mrs. Gandy turned and looked me in the eye.

"Folks not harmonizing in your world, little girl?" she asked. I felt like Mrs. Gandy was somebody I wanted to lean against, so I could think about things and sort them out.

"Nobody's even *trying*. It used to be that all the bad stuff was on television or in the newspaper, and I just didn't look at it. I used to close my eyes every night when the news came on. But now it's even going on in the sixth grade! Everybody hates somebody else." I felt like I was making a speech, but Mrs. Gandy was looking at me like she didn't mind hearing it, so I kept going. "Nobody listens to anybody else. And I'm not much better," I said. "It seems like sometimes we all just stop *trying*. Or else we work on it for a little while, and then forget and go back to doing our own thing."

"Doing your own thing," Mrs. Gandy said. She played some deep chords. "Now Amanda, my girl, don't you know that's what harmony *is*? Every note is doing its own thing." She played a bunch of different notes separately. "But when it all comes together—" She played a string of chords and looked at me. That lady could make a piano do anything, even sound like it had all the answers to life's questions.

"Harmony?" I said.

She threw her head back. "Harmony, honey!" she shouted, and now she was playing like the piano was on fire and nothing but fast playing would put it out, and I twirled on my piano stool, laughing and clapping in time to the music. When I stopped the stool with my feet I had my back to the piano, and once I could see straight again I saw Sporty standing in the doorway.

"I ought to go get my guitar right now," he said. "Yes,

sir, I ought to be down here playing the guitar with you, and singing." Then he walked away.

Mrs. Gandy laughed with me and said, "Anyway, honey, your job is to keep trying to play your own harmony." At the end of my lesson, she said, "Now, I'll see you here next week, same time as always."

Now *that* was harmony—knowing that Mrs. Gandy would be there the next week, and the week after that. In the same place, at the same time.

Mom had to take Laura to the dentist that afternoon, and she'd told me she'd probably be a little late picking me up after my lesson. I sat on the front steps to wait. A lot of the black kids walked to school from their houses, and usually some of them stayed late to talk and hang out, so there were lots of people around.

"Amanda Adams!" Henry Bailey came over to me. "What are you still doing here?"

I couldn't help but shiver a little bit. I had almost decided that he was all right, but his oral report had changed that. Besides, he was one of the boys who hung out at Sporty's office and gave me funny looks.

"I had piano today," I said. "And my mom's coming to pick me up."

"Well, let's go practice our boost, girl," he said. "This is what Miss G. would call a golden opportunity."

"My mom should be here pretty soon," I said. I looked down the street. No car.

"Oh, come on," Henry said. He grabbed my arm and

pulled me after him down the steps. "Let's go try it out. That's the only way we're going to know that we can do it."

I shook his hand off my arm. As we walked to the obstacle course I said, "Henry, do you hate white people?"

He didn't answer. When we got to the obstacle course, he stopped and looked at me. "Girl," he said, "let's just try to get over this Wall."

The Wall looked even higher than usual. "I don't know if I can do this," I said.

"Only one way *to* know," Henry said. He laced his fingers together and stood about two feet away from the Wall. "Go get you a running start, and let's boost."

I set my briefcase down on the leaves and walked a few steps away. "I've got my oxfords on today," I warned him, but Henry just shook his hands once to tell me to get on with it.

I took a deep breath, ran toward Henry, felt myself going up and up, then hit the Wall. It got me right in the top of the chest, and I came back down and landed on my rear end. I couldn't get a breath. Neither could Henry; he was laughing too hard.

"Girl, you'll be flat-chested forever, now," he said. "*Whomp!* I never saw anybody hit anything so hard."

"Shut . . . up."

He rolled over in the leaves, still laughing. I finally was able to stand up, brushed the leaves off my pants, and picked up my briefcase to go.

"Don't leave now!" Henry said. "We almost got it! Another inch or two, and you'd have been over that Wall."

"Well, I guess it's a good thing it didn't work," I said. "If I *had* gotten over it, I probably would have killed myself landing on the other side, with nobody there to catch me."

Henry stopped laughing. "Well, now, that's a fact," he said. "I didn't figure on that. But anyway, we know now that we *can* do it. All we need is two people up there to wait for you, to haul your skinny ass over."

I looked at the Wall and said, "It reminds me of a story we learned in Sunday school—about Joshua marching around Jericho, and the walls of the city falling down."

Henry looked at the Wall. "I'd like to knock it down into the dust and dance on the pieces. I'm beginning to take this Wall real *personal.*"

"We'll beat it," I told him. "Just don't forget that you need *me* to help you." I looked at him hard.

"Amanda!"

I turned around. Laura was walking across the playground, with an extremely weird look on her face. When I turned back and saw the look on Henry's face, my blood ran cold.

CHAPTER 21

"My mom's here," I told Henry. "I've gotta go."

He kept watching Laura. He looked confused, like he wasn't sure if he was mad or scared.

"Amanda," Laura said, as she came up to where we were standing, "are you ready to go? Mom's waiting out front."

Henry looked down at his feet. "Laura, this is Henry. Henry, this is my sister, Laura," I said. Henry looked back up.

"What's the matter with you?" I asked him.

"Nothing," he mumbled, and he started to walk away.

"Well, I'll see you tomorrow," I said.

Henry turned back around and said to Laura, "I wasn't trying to *rape* nobody."

"What's that supposed to mean?" I yelled. "Has everybody gone crazy?"

"Let's go," Laura said, and by the time we got to the car we were fighting.

"Why did you have to go and do that?" I climbed into the backseat and slammed the door shut. "I have to sit in front of him every day of my life."

She got in the front seat and turned to face me. "I didn't *do* anything!"

"Well, of course you did. You made him feel bad, didn't you?"

"What's going on?" Mom asked. We shut up. Then Laura finally said, "I apparently hurt Amanda's little friend's feelings. But I didn't *do* anything, or *say* anything! He must be the most sensitive soul on the face of the planet."

Henry Bailey, a sensitive soul? I almost laughed out loud. But then I remembered that look on his face.

When we got home and Mom had gone down the hall, Laura said, "I'm sorry, Amanda. I didn't mean to hurt his feelings. But when I got out of the car, those kids hanging around in front of the school said, 'If you're looking for that little white girl, Henry Bailey made her go with him back over there.' "

"He didn't *make* me," I said, but I wasn't mad anymore. I just felt sad. And I didn't know what to do next.

"I know how you feel," Laura said. "Sometimes it's like I'm walking a tightrope, and I get so tired of having to watch my feet so that I don't slip and fall." She shook her head. "At my school, sometimes the dumbest thing will set people off. Like yesterday that idiotic Roger Newman was walking down the hall, and a black guy just brushed past him. That happens all the time when we're changing classes, but Roger acted like he'd been insulted, or something, and he tried to start a fight." She stopped and closed her eyes for a moment. "It's hard on the old nerves, knowing that people are so jumpy."

It was *very* hard on the old nerves. I hadn't realized that Laura was having a tough time, too. After dinner, she tossed her hair behind her shoulders and looked at Dad. I could see that she wanted to pick a fight.

"You know," she said, "Timothy Warren wrote an excellent opinion column for the school paper, about the problems of desegregation, but the faculty adviser wouldn't let him print it. He called the column 'inflammatory.' So you know what Timothy did? He left a blank space where the column should have been, and wrote underneath it that desegregation in Windsor County is exactly like the Vietnam War—a bunch of old men cooked up a plan, and then sent the young people out to do the real work. We're not allowed to express our opinions about it. Timothy said the old men should get out of the way and let us work desegregation out for ourselves. He said they haven't done a very good job of handling things up to now, and it was time to let the youth of America take over."

"God forbid," Dad said.

"Hey! When everybody was talking me into being desegregated, all I heard was stuff about pioneers and making the world a better place," I said. "Nobody told me it was going to be like war."

"Well, sometimes it takes a little blood, and sweat, and pain to make the world a better place," Dad said. "Sometimes it gets even worse than that. Sometimes high-school punks start thinking they're smart enough to run the world."

Laura whirled out of the room. "I can't talk to you," she said.

Mom and Dad looked at me. "The whole world's gone nuts," I said.

Henry wouldn't speak to me at all the next day. On Thursday Miss Gohagan gave us a pop quiz in science and graded them during lunch. When she passed them back to us, Henry didn't even look over my shoulder to see what grade I'd gotten.

I hoped he would get over being mad during the weekend. I actually missed Henry.

It felt weird.

"Now, Amanda, I am concerned about your progress," Mrs. Gandy said, "and I think we need to have us a little conversation."

I had just finished playing my song straight through without a single mistake. It was the same song I'd been working on for two weeks (another one with no sharps or flats). I couldn't believe Mrs. Gandy wasn't thrilled.

She sat on her piano stool, looking at me. "You know I suggested last week that you try a new song in your book. Now, you played that song just fine, but what I want to know is, when are you going to try something a little more difficult? You told me you loved 'Jesu, Joy of Man's Desiring.' Why haven't you started working on it?"

"Well, I just wanted to be able to play this one perfectly before I started on something new," I said.

"All right, then, that other one's perfect. Let's turn these pages over and try 'Jesu,' now."

I looked at it and sort of froze up. It had so many fast notes right there at the beginning. I knew I was about to make a fool of myself.

I said, "I don't *want* to play 'Jesu.' Can't you just let me pick the songs I want to do?"

I used the tone of voice that my mother hates, and that I hate, too, if you want to know the truth.

Mrs. Gandy kept looking at me with her dark, dark eyes, and she didn't get huffy back. Her tone of voice changed, too, but not in a bad way. She said, "Amanda, you are mixed up, and I can help you get unmixed. You think it's better to play something simple, and easy as one plus one equals two, and not make any mistakes. But the fact of the matter is, you are going to miss out on a whole lot of living if you don't start subtracting, and multiplying, and yes! doing long division, too. When you move on to the harder things, Amanda, there's fun, and there's joy, and there's a whole lot of satisfaction. You don't want to miss out on that! Now, I am not going to sit here and tell you what you will and will not play. You look through this book a minute, and you decide."

Tucked into the back of the book was my old sheet music for "My Grandfather's Clock." Mrs. Gandy pulled it out and put it beside the book of music she'd given me. "And here's old 'Grandfather's Clock,'" she said. "That's a good song, too. We're going to have a school recital before too much longer, Amanda, and whatever you decide on today, that's what we'll start working on for the recital. There'll be plenty of time for you to change your mind, if you like, but you just look through there and see what you think."

127

Mrs. Gandy rolled her stool away and started to make some notations in her gradebook. I didn't actually get a grade for my piano lessons, but Mrs. Gandy sent home a progress report when report cards came out.

I looked at the music book. "Jesu, Joy of Man's Desiring" would mean weeks of banging on the piano and sounding terrible. Why waste the time? "My Grandfather's Clock" sounded even better lately, because I'd learned how to play it with my whole body. It was by far my best playing. I looked up at Mrs. Gandy. She was watching me over the gradebook.

I knew what would make her happy. What would make her happy would make me completely miserable. I almost felt like crying. " 'Jesu,' " I said, putting "My Grandfather's Clock" in the book again. And then I almost *did* cry, because Mrs. Gandy looked so glad that I almost couldn't stand to see it. It was like staring straight at the sun.

She looked up at the ceiling. "Lord, I *knew* this child had good sense!" she said.

CHAPTER 22

There were some boys hanging around Sporty's door again that afternoon, and as I got closer Henry Bailey came out. I said, "Henry!" It came out kind of weak.

As usual, whatever was going on in Sporty's office got real hush-hush. Henry walked toward me. "What you want, Amanda Adams?" he asked.

"Let's practice our boost again, before my mom gets here," I said. I knew she was probably outside waiting, but I wanted to make sure everything was okay between Henry and me.

He laced his fingers together right there in the hallway. "Well, let's go," he said.

I looked behind me. Mrs. Gandy was still in her classroom, so I put my briefcase down and backed away to get a running start. I ran toward him, put my foot in his hands, and then I panicked and ducked, throwing my arms around his shoulders to keep from falling.

"What in the world kind of trick was that?" Henry said. He let me go. "You act like you hadn't ever done that boost in your life."

"Look," I said, pointing up at the ceiling. The basement

129

ceilings weren't nearly as high as the ceilings in the rest of the school, and there were pipes running back and forth across them. If I had done the boost like I was supposed to, I'd have probably cracked my head wide open on one of them.

"Henry, what you letting that white girl hug on your neck for?" Joenathan asked.

"Shut up, toad, we was practicing on our boost, and Amanda Adams is afraid of a little concussion. Girl, you already got brain damage, so I don't see what the problem is."

By this time most of the boys had come out of Sporty's office and were looking at us. I picked up my briefcase and decided to exit, stage left. As I walked away, I heard guitar music again, and a man's voice singing, the words slow and drawn out:

> I used to think I had it all figured out
> But now I don't see it so clear,
> No, I ain't crazy
> But I can see it from here.

I stopped and turned around. "Is that *Sporty* singing?" I asked Henry.

"Yes, girl, it's Sporty. Now get on out of here and leave us men be."

"Why's he sound so sad?"

For a second I thought Henry was going to ignore me and walk away, but then he said, "He's singing the blues, girl. Don't you know that? Sporty can play some blues, 'cause he's had trouble in his own life. He's playing next Saturday in a drink joint at Twenty-eighth Street—that's how good he is, and that's why he's practicin' so much."

I stood in the hallway with my briefcase in my hand and my knee socks down around my ankles. If music was something to eat, I would like songs that tasted like fancy desserts, with chocolate and whipped cream. Sporty's songs would have tasted like salt and vinegar.

Henry said, "Get on home, girl, and don't you be worrying about Sporty. He just plays for us sometimes, when he feels like it."

"You know," I said, "if he'd just go talk to Mrs. Gandy, and take some lessons from her, he would probably sound a whole lot better. She could teach him some *happier* songs, too."

Henry looked at me like I was a total idiot. Then he turned and went into Sporty's office, so I picked up my stupid briefcase and went home.

October 12 was Henry's birthday, and he brought in a cake for our whole class. I saw him that morning as I got off the bus. Henry was walking up the sidewalk toward the front door of the school carrying a glass cake plate with a cover over it. He was walking really slow and careful. It was funny to see Henry carrying that birthday cake like it was a baby, or a bomb, or something, but not the kind of funny that makes you want to laugh.

I ran ahead of him to hold the door open, but he walked by me like I wasn't there. He acted like that cake was so extra-special that doors would just automatically open for him wherever he carried it. It was a good cake, too—yellow, with chocolate icing. We ate it after lunch and before *Huckleberry Finn.*

"Did you make this cake yourself, Henry?" Miss Gohagan asked.

He looked disgusted, like he was much too manly to ever try to bake a cake. "Naw," he said, licking icing off the side of his little white plastic fork. "My mama made the cake, and my aunt made the icing. They can't neither one of them make a thing by theyself."

After we had Henry's cake, Amy Voorhees read Chapter Twenty-six of *Huck Finn,* but at the end of that chapter it was the part where Huck was slipping down the ladder to try and find a place to hide the bag of money he'd taken from the fake king and the fake duke. We were all glad that she went right on reading Chapter Twenty-seven, but when Miss Gohagan realized what Amy had done she said that it wasn't fair, that we should let the tension build until the next day.

"Turn in your history textbook to page fifty-two," Miss Gohagan said. "Read the two paragraphs under the heading 'Heroes and Villains.' "

I read the paragraphs, and while I waited for everybody else to finish I stared out the window. I saw myself wearing a long black skirt with a white satin blouse. I tapped the music stand in front of me with my conductor's baton and said, "Ready, please. Once more, the *Symphony in Desegregation.*"

"What? We got to play that same old song again?" It was the first violinist, Henry Bailey, speaking. If anything happened to Amanda, the conductor, it would be Henry's job to lead the orchestra.

Amanda didn't answer him; she looked at him until Henry brought his violin up and prepared to play. Then she coolly lifted the baton. "This piece must be played very loudly, and all together. *Fortissimo, de facto!*"

The opening notes of *Symphony in Desegregation*—an original composition by Amanda Adams—filled the rehearsal hall. Darlene played clarinet. Amy played second violin beside Henry. Henry's sister played flute, Kathy played viola, and David played bass drum. Kyle held the cymbals, waiting for Amanda to cue him to clash them together. The *Symphony in Desegregation* had a lot of cymbals in it, and they were the only instrument that didn't play constantly from beginning to end. Joenathan, John Williams, and some of the other boys played trumpets and saxophones. Sporty Deane sat next to the bass drum, playing guitar. Of course Mrs. Gandy played piano, and Miss Gohagan played harp. Her harp didn't have strings on it, though. Instead she strummed her fingers across pages from her red booklet.

I turned away from the window and looked down at my history book. What a strange, mixed-up orchestra! And I had forgotten to imagine Jackie playing in it. If I was the conductor, she should have been first violin. But it was hard to think of Henry playing second fiddle to anybody. Ha—I'd made a joke. As usual, nobody enjoyed it but me.

Two days later it was my turn to read another chapter, and the next day Henry Bailey read Chapter Thirty-one. He was reading along in a kind of bored tone of voice like he always did, but then Huck Finn started arguing with himself about whether or not he ought to turn Jim in, since he was a runaway slave and it was wrong to help a runaway slave. Henry seemed like he was getting interested in the story, and he started to read with a little more *feeling.* Henry read about Huck thinking he was committing a sin by helping Jim run away, and that he was going to go to hell for it. So Huck decided to write a letter to Miss Watson and tell her where Jim was. He felt better right away, until he reminded himself of all the good times he and Jim had had together, and he thought about how good Jim had been to him, and finally Huck said to himself,

> . . . I'd got to decide, forever, betwixt two things, and I knowed it. I studied a minute, sort of holding my breath, and then says to myself:
> "All right, then, I'll *go* to hell!"—

and Huck tore the letter up!

Henry looked up from the book with a big grin on his face, because as soon as he read that, our whole class just busted out cheering and clapping. For a few minutes we had that team spirit that Miss Gohagan was always talking about. And Miss Gohagan understood, even if she did look a little bit surprised. She didn't make us do extra math for having an outburst.

CHAPTER 23

 "Henry, you aren't working on your journal," Miss Gohagan said.

"Yes, I am, too," Henry said, real fast. "Amanda Adams is interviewing me, and I already interviewed her, Miss Gohagan, so you just go on down the line and fuss at somebody else."

I couldn't believe he didn't get in trouble for smart talk. Not to mention lying. "You did not interview me," I whispered after Miss Gohagan had moved away.

Henry opened his journal and showed me a page that said, INTERVIEW WITH AMANDA ADAMS.

"You must have made it all up," I said, "because you never interviewed me."

"I didn't have to," he said. "I already know all about you. I put down here that you have a sister that looks exactly like you, and that you take piano lessons, and that you can do a mean layup. I put down that you jump higher than anybody in this class, and that your favorite color is green. Any fool would know that, because you wear that green vest *all* the time and I sit right behind you and have to look at it. Plus, I read what all you told Beastle when she interviewed you."

I was impressed. I was also kind of happy, because he'd said nice things about me. "Neat. Did you interview anybody else like that?"

"I got an interview in here with Sporty," he said. He flipped a couple of pages, and one of his newspaper clippings fell out. He swung sideways so that both feet went way up in the air and grabbed it before it hit the floor. He handed me his journal. "I asked him a few questions," Henry said, "but mostly I just wrote down what I know."

INTERVIEW WITH ALBERT SPORTY DEANE, it said. Henry had written that Sporty had been the janitor at East Windsor Elementary since 1959. He told about how Sporty wrote blues songs and sang them on the weekends. Sporty's favorite food was turkey and dressing. His best friend was Clarence Garver, who lived across the street and drove a Greyhound bus for a living. One summer Sporty had ridden with Clarence from Windsor to Memphis, Tennessee, and back.

"That's a good interview," I said. "Now I need to finish yours. I already know your birthday's in October. What was the date? October twelfth. Okay, so what's your favorite color?"

"Black," Henry said, and he held up his fist in a Black Power salute.

"Favorite season?"

"Summer vacation, fool."

"If you could be anything in the world, what would you like to be?"

Henry crossed his arms and looked out the window. I waited. Finally I looked out the window, too. Spaghetti Eddie was walking down the sidewalk away from the school—I recognized his brown hat. Henry never did give me an answer.

The days were beginning to get a lot cooler. Sporty had stopped wearing his tan work clothes; now he wore dark gray work pants and a matching long-sleeved shirt to school.

It was perfect weather for running around outside. One afternoon at recess I kept looking up, because the sky was blue with no clouds in sight. The trees around EWE were dropping yellow leaves that made the ground seem sunny, too. The air was crisp, and full of the good smell of tobacco from Galt Brothers. Miss Gohagan could tell we felt a little bit wild, so she got us started on a big game of dodgeball, to use up some of our energy.

The longer we played, the warmer it got. Some of the boys took off their jackets and threw them on the ground. Then the rest of us took ours off, and the pile of jackets got bigger. It was so beautiful outside, and we were having such a great time, that Miss Gohagan had to yell to get us to head back inside. *"Now,* people!" she said. "Get your jackets back on, and march!" She turned and started walking away as we ran for the pile.

It was sort of like another game, with everybody digging through the jackets to find the right one. We yelled and pushed each other, and then Henry (of course) started being silly. He put on Blake's jacket, which was too small for him. His skinny wrists hung out the ends of the sleeves. Then Blake put on David's jacket, and it was way too big for him.

137

Everybody started putting on somebody else's jacket, and we would never have gone back to class if Miss Gohagan hadn't come back to get us.

"Whose jacket am I wearing?" I asked. "And where's mine?"

"That's mine you've got on," a soft voice said. It was Marcella Bailey.

She smiled at me. The sleeves were too long on me, but the jacket was warm and smelled like something sweet—like dried flowers. We both laughed, and I gave it back. Amy Voorhees threw mine to me, and I pulled it on as we walked back toward school.

"Hey, Amanda Adams!" Henry said. "Let's practice that boost."

I couldn't resist. It was such a great day, I wanted to jump and see how high I could go. It was damp outside, and my foot left a mudprint on Henry's palm. He chased me back to the school so he could wipe it off on my jacket, but when he caught up to me, he let me get away.

"Now, what's going on up there?" Henry asked. He was staring at the front of the school. A group of big black kids—five or six of them—were standing in front of EWE with their arms linked. They looked like they must be ninth- and tenth-graders from East Windsor High, the school next door. They were swaying back and forth and chanting something. It was scary.

Henry was looking at me. I could tell that he knew exactly what I was thinking.

"Ain't nobody going to mess with you," he said, disgusted. "They're just protesting, is all." He started walking toward them, and I followed.

"What are they protesting?"

"That's what I'm gonna find out."

I could hear the words now:

We don't care what we been told.
The Mighty Tigers won't be sold.

"Who are the Mighty Tigers?" I asked Henry.

"That was the name of the East Windsor High School teams. The Mighty Tigers."

Mrs. Gandy came down the front steps from the school. "Now, what is this?" she asked. I couldn't believe how brave she was.

One of the protesters stepped forward and waved his fist in the air. He got right in Mrs. Gandy's face. "They told us when school started that we're no longer the Mighty Tigers," he said. "Told us we had to vote on a new school mascot and school colors. Now they went and just *gave* us a new school song! All because we got white kids in class with us now."

He stood so close to Mrs. Gandy that I could see flecks of spit hitting her in the face. I stepped backward onto Henry's foot. He pushed me away.

Mrs. Gandy crossed her arms in front of her chest. "Well," she said, "didn't those white students lose their school, and their mascot, and their school colors, too?"

"Yeah, but that's no reason to change ours. Principal says

we got to be neutral, but he's a white man, and we don't have to listen to a thing that man says."

"And tell me this, Raymond, why in the world are you over here at the elementary school with your big, bad protest?"

"Principal's over here meeting with Mr. Harrison." The more Raymond had to explain himself to Mrs. Gandy, the less scary he seemed.

"This is no way to handle your frustrations," she said. "Coming over here to this school and making a fuss in front of the younger children! Why don't you elect a committee to talk to Mr. Vandenburg about these issues? Or write up a petition and circulate it—show him how much support you've got behind you. Do things the right way, and you'll get a lot more done."

Mrs. Gandy turned to go back inside the school. She stopped and turned back to Raymond. "But you're fighting a losing battle here, honey," she said. "There's no reason in the world to spend your time on things that don't matter. I know you feel like the traditions of your school are being destroyed, but that's what this thing is all *about,* Raymond. We're stamping out the bad traditions. Some good traditions are going to get stomped in the process, but that's the way it is."

The big kids stood around like they weren't sure what to do next, and I turned around and pulled Henry's arm.

"We'd better get to class," I said. "We're going to get in trouble."

We ran to Miss Gohagan's room, and sure enough she'd

left Henry and me five math problems to work. I looked at the problems, but I thought about Mrs. Gandy. She had no fear. She went ahead and acted like those protesters were going to do exactly what she told them. I wondered if I would ever learn to be like that. If I was going to be a conductor, I had to get used to telling people what to do. I had to work with a whole group and not hide behind anybody. I wasn't sure I'd ever be able to do that.

CHAPTER 24

I had outgrown my last year's good winter coat, so one Saturday Mom took me to Sears to pick out a new one. And for once in my life, I found a coat that I *loved*. It was deep blue, and it felt just like real suede, and it was a *maxi* coat. I walked around Sears with the coat on, swaying so that the heavy material hit my legs. I felt like a bell.

"Mom, I *love* this one," I said. "It makes me feel so *cool*."

She turned away from a rack of ski jackets. Her eyes looked right through me, like I was a stranger, and then she really saw me. "Oh, Amanda," she said. "I almost didn't recognize you, you look so tall and grown up." I could tell she didn't exactly like that, but she bought the coat for me anyway.

Jackie came over after church on Sunday, and I showed her my new coat. She liked it, but what she really wanted to do was sneak into Laura's room and look at *her* clothes. "Does Laura ever wear a choker?" Jackie asked.

"Yeah, she makes them herself," I said. "She's got all sorts of different little pins and things to put on them, and she buys black velvet ribbon from the Piecegoods Store, so it looks like she has about a hundred different ones."

"We made a rule in my class," Jackie said, her eyes shining like they do when she's up to something, "that all the girls had to wear a choker on Friday, and anybody who didn't we didn't talk to *all day.*"

"But what if somebody just forgot?" I asked. I could easily imagine that I would be the one person who'd forget to wear one, and how terrible I'd feel. "Anyway, that's cliquish, and *we* aren't allowed to have cliques!"

Jackie was already laughing at something else that she wanted to tell me. "We have this teacher at our school who wears hot pink frosted lipstick. She teaches fourth grade. So we made up a song about her. You wanta hear it?"

"Okay."

Jackie snapped her fingers and shook her head while she chanted the words of the song:

Hot Pink	{snap—snap—snap}
Rinky-Dink,	{snap—snap—snap}
Well, I think	{snap—snap—snap}
That you stink.	{snap . . . snap}

Then she laughed so hard she had to lie down on the floor.

Maybe I'd have laughed, too, if I'd been there when it was thought of, but since I wasn't, and since I didn't even know the teacher she was making fun of, I couldn't really get into the spirit of it.

"Man, you're no fun at all anymore," Jackie said, as if she knew how I felt, almost. "You're ewwwww."

That wasn't funny. EWE was my school now.

"It's only ewww because you're not there with me," I said.

Jackie held her nose and said, *"Eeewww."*

I wanted to tell her shut up. Instead, I sat down on the piano bench and played the first couple of bars of "Jesu, Joy of Man's Desiring," to show off. I was beginning to like playing it, except for one part at the beginning that I sometimes flubbed.

Jackie's eyes sparkled. "Hey, I heard that there are riots going on downtown at the high school. Can you see them from your school?"

"There aren't any riots going on downtown. Who made up that rumor?" I didn't feel like telling her about the ninth- and tenth-grade protesters.

Jackie sat down beside me so hard that the bench moved sideways, and that made both of us laugh. It felt good to laugh about the same thing for a change. "At my school, we're always hearing rumors about riots and sit-ins and stuff," she said.

"Well, if there were any, I'm sure *I'd* have heard about it," I said. "And I told you there wasn't anything going on in Sporty's office—he just plays music and sings."

"So what's Beastle been up to lately?" Jackie asked.

Jackie still loved me to make up stories about Beastle. I couldn't believe she hadn't gotten tired of hearing them.

"Oh, I don't know," I said. I thought for about ten seconds. "She went to the doctor, and he fixed her. Now she isn't slimy anymore."

"No!" Jackie said. "My lunch group likes to hear the slimy, disgusting Beastle stories."

144

I felt cold. She was telling all her private school friends my Beastle stories? I played the piano while I thought about that. Jackie wanted Beastle to be something awful. She wanted riots—she *wanted* it to be *ewwww.* All of those private school kids probably *loved* hearing terrible things about desegregation. It probably made them feel great. I was probably making them even more prejudiced than they already were.

I shook my head, and said, "Let's pretend that I'm Mrs. Gandy, my music teacher, and you're me. Place your fingers on the keyboard, little girl, and let's see those shoulders *move.*"

I wasn't making fun of Mrs. Gandy. She was the only person on planet Earth who could talk me into trying to play a hard song. I'd told Jackie all about her.

Jackie pretended to be deaf and stupid, and she looked at me with her mouth hanging open and said, "Whuuut?"

"That's it, now you're playing," I said. I put my hands on her shoulders. "Get into it, now. That's the way."

Jackie stopped pretending to be the stupidest piano student in the world and said, "I don't see how you can stand it, Amanda." Then she got off the bench and walked over to the record player. She started flipping through the forty-fives.

"How I stand what?" I asked. I was trying the beginning part of "Jesu, Joy of Man's Desiring" again. I concentrated on getting it right.

"Having to sit next to a fat, sweaty nigger for piano lessons."

145

I stopped playing. The "Tornado in D" swept through my head like an ugly yellow thunderstorm.

Jackie probably never knew what hit her. But when she ran out of my house she had a big red slap mark on her face, and my palm turned white, then it turned red, and it felt like I'd smacked a steel wall. It felt very satisfying for about two minutes.

Then I stopped hearing the "Tornado in D," and I couldn't believe what I'd done.

CHAPTER 25

I felt like a tiny dried-up old bone sitting all by myself in a desert. Mom and Laura were busy yakking away in the kitchen, so I went outside and dragged a big chunk of firewood over to the Secret Garden side of the house.

I sat there and stared at the house. I wanted to think. But after about five minutes I realized that I didn't want to think, after all. So I looked for something to do.

"I'm getting ready to go out to a site and take some measurements," Dad said. "You want to go with me?"

Dad was working on a house in a new subdivision not far from where we lived. I rode with him in his big blue truck with the tool chest in the back. The yard at the new house was red dirt, with a couple of spindly pine trees left on it. The foundation had been poured, and the framing had started. There were studs up, but no walls yet, and no roof. Dad went off to take his measurements, and I walked around inside. The place smelled like fresh wood and rain.

At first I went through the doorways and pretended that the house was finished and I was the interior designer, planning where the sofa and other furniture would go. Then I pretended that I had died in that house and came back as a ghost to haunt it. After that I didn't use the doorways anymore. Instead, I pretended that I was passing through solid walls as I went from room to room.

I thought it would probably be easy to be a ghost.

That night I called Jackie's house, and when Jackie answered the phone, I jumped right in. "I'm sorry I slapped you, Jackie," I said. "It was uncalled for."

There was no sound from Jackie, except a little faint click like she'd knocked the phone against her teeth.

"I guess we'll never be able to be best friends again," I said. I waited for her to tell me I was being crazy, but she still didn't answer. "It's too bad, because we've been best friends since first grade, and I thought we'd be best friends forever."

I thought that I could hear her breathing, and I imagined her sitting at the other end of the phone line, with tears running down her cheeks.

"But I guess you can't be my best friend if I'm going to go around slapping your face, and I can't be your best friend if you're going to say hateful things about Mrs. Gandy. You've never even met Mrs. Gandy. It doesn't make sense for you to say mean things about her and call her ugly words."

There was a rattling sound from Jackie's end of the phone, and Jackie's mother said, "Hello?"

"Hello?" I said. "Mrs. Charles? I thought I was talking to Jackie."

"No, dear," Mrs. Charles said. "She put the phone down

and left it—I thought she'd just left it off the hook. I think she's in her bedroom. Do you want me to get her for you?"

"No, thank you," I said. "Just tell her I said good-bye."

It probably wasn't quite cold enough yet for me to wear my new coat, but it's really hard to not wear new stuff when it's right there, hanging in your closet. Besides, it made me feel better to wear something new. Now that Jackie and I were probably never going to speak to each other again, I needed that. It worked, too, because when Laura saw it on Monday morning while we were waiting for the bus, she said, "Wow. I feel like I'm waiting for the bus with Cher."

But once I got to school and had to hang my coat up in the back of the classroom, I felt sad again. Even though Jackie had never been to this school with me, I could feel that she was more gone now than ever. I felt like an empty winter field, with nothing but old dried-up stalks left sticking out of the frozen dirt.

At least we had something special that day, to help take my mind off my fight with Jackie. Amy Voorhees had brought in a special project. Her father is a brain surgeon, and she had brought a brain to school in a shoe box.

"Girl, did you ride the *school bus* with that brain setting in your lap?" Henry Bailey asked her. But she hadn't—her mother had driven her.

"It looks like a gray meat loaf, getting ready to be baked," Marcella said. She put her finger out like she wanted to touch the brain (it was in a plastic bag), but then she put her hand behind her back.

"Beastle, your brain *is* a meat loaf," Henry said. He looked in the box again. "Dag, girl, now you went and ruined meat loaf for me! I'll never eat that mess again."

I looked at Marcella, and we both busted out laughing.

I called Jackie again that afternoon after I got home, but she wouldn't talk to me. I knew she was a pain in the neck. I knew she was mean. But it didn't matter—I wanted her back. I missed her. I had been going to EWE long enough to have almost gotten used to not seeing her as much, but as soon as we stopped speaking, I felt like I had that first day I'd found out that she was going to private school—like the world was coming to an end.

One night, before I did my math homework, I borrowed a ruler and a sheet of typing paper from Dad's desk in the basement. Dad was busy at the kitchen table with Laura, trying to teach her how to use a slide rule. Dad told Laura that once she learned how, she could use it to find the answers to hard math problems.

Too bad there wasn't a slide rule that gave the answers to hard *life* problems. Miss Gohagan and I could both buy one. Her red booklet didn't seem to be helping much. I had looked in it again one day. Teachers were supposed to emphasize reading and music. "Play music of all types, both songs that are popular with black children and those that are popular with white children." What good would that do?

I drew a picture of a ruler on the piece of typing paper. I put in all the little marks for inches and quarter inches, and all the numbers. Then I wrote: "Don't you think it's time for us to get our hair measured? Check yes ☐ or no ☐. Please return this note to me on Sunday!" I addressed an envelope to Jackie, and Mom mailed it for me.

By Sunday I was kind of wound up. I was one of the first kids to get to Sunday school, so I sat in one of the little wooden chairs around the long wooden table and chewed on my thumbnail and waited.

Jackie came in with a group of other kids. As usual, they were talking about stuff that was going on at New Canaan Academy. Jennifer and I were always kind of left out, but today I decided to make a move and do *something*. So when Miss Elaine left the room to find some Magic Markers, I tipped my wooden chair onto its back legs and hung on to the edge of the table with my fingertips. I sort of seesawed back and forth like I was really cool while I sang a few lines of "Rockin' Robin." Two or three people laughed, and Jennifer said, "Amanda, you're nuts."

I didn't look at Jackie, so I didn't know if she had laughed or not. Then my fingers slipped off the edge of the table. My chair fell backward with a huge crash.

The room got totally quiet after my crash. I lay there in my chair, waiting for Miss Elaine to come storming in the door. That's when Jackie threw my note back to me. It landed on my chest. I didn't even get up first—I unfolded it right then. She had checked the "no" box.

I lay there staring up at the string Miss Elaine had tied across the room. It had construction paper butterflies hanging from it, with heart-shaped wings and pipe cleaner bodies. I think I'd still be lying there now if Jennifer hadn't given me her hand to help me up. Jennifer is the type of girl who doesn't say a whole lot and doesn't have a bubbly personality, but I guess since she had listened in Sunday school all those years she had learned more about being helpful and kind than Jackie and me put together. I asked her to sit with me during the worship service, and she did. She had dark red hair that she usually pulled back and tied at her neck into a ponytail. Her skin was pale, except for the freckles across her nose. She would probably look very good in an emerald green bridesmaid dress. Emerald green was my favorite color.

Things went from bad to worse. Miss Gohagan took us to the gym to play basketball. She gave us two balls—one for the girls to play half-court on one side, and one for the boys to play half-court on the other—and then she left to go to the teachers' lounge.

We played and were having a pretty good time. I enjoyed it because the teams weren't so huge and the boys couldn't hog the ball the whole time. The only problem we had was when we had to chase the ball onto each other's court.

Then the clicking started.

Robin Sutton snapped her fingers at Holly Johnson, just to get her attention, but then they both laughed and started clicking at each other every time they ran past each other. Amy and Carolyn got in on it, too. I thought they must have all gone crazy, and I concentrated on getting in position to make a layup. But I couldn't seem to get the ball through the net.

The heavy gym doors clanged shut, and Miss Gohagan

came in. Our time was up, and she walked toward our side of the court with her hand up to call us to the door. And that's when Darlene Jeffries said, "Miss Gohagan! Make these white girls stop snapping their fingers!"

Her voice echoed in the gymnasium.

Miss Gohagan's voice was cold. "Line up, sixth-graders!" she said. "Let's move it!"

We left the basketballs rolling on the court, and we moved it. Nobody said a word as we walked back to class. Carolyn stopped at the rest room to change her clothes, and I thought that if I were her, I'd never come back out.

One at a time, Miss Gohagan took every girl in our class into the hall for a "talk." The boys were doing everything they could to find out what was going on, but nobody would tell them. I didn't even know if all the black girls knew. By the time it was my turn, my palms were sweaty and my stomach was upset. I closed the classroom door behind me and walked over to Miss Gohagan. She stood with her arms crossed, waiting for me.

"Amanda, I understand that you have been involved in this, but that you were not one of the girls actually using the secret code today," she said. "I hope that means that you already realize how wrong it was to band together and exclude the black girls from your group."

"Yes, I knew it was wrong," I said. My eyes burned, and I stopped talking until I could be sure I wasn't going to cry. "When it first started, it seemed like a good way to have friends." I looked up at her and then back down at my oxfords.

"It's not a good way to have friends when that way involves grouping together by skin color, or eye color, or by what side of town you live on," Miss Gohagan said. "You should form friendships based on things you have in common on the inside, not on the outside."

I thought about that as I walked back to my desk. Maybe the only reason I wanted Jackie to be my best friend was because of things on the outside. When you got right down to it, we sure didn't have a lot in common on the inside.

Henry Bailey was sitting in my desk, waiting for me. "Come on, Amanda Adams," he said. "What's going on out there in that hallway? You can tell me about it—you know how tight we are!"

"Miss Gohagan is telling us about how to get along together," I told him.

He slowly got up and moved back to his own desk. "Is that all?" he said. "Miss G. got a one-track mind, I believe. Well, it ain't nothing to cry over," he added, looking at my face.

"I'm not crying," I said, gritting my teeth. I turned toward the windows so the rest of the class couldn't see me. "I think I must be getting a cold." I looked in my purse, but I knew there wasn't a Kleenex in it. I gulped, and said, "*Why* don't I carry Kleenex with me?" Then I looked up.

Henry was watching me with a worried crease in his forehead. He had his arm stuck out in front of me, offering me the sleeve of his blue plaid flannel shirt.

We looked at each other for a second, and then we both busted out laughing. And I sat at my desk and laughed, with tears rolling down my cheeks, and I couldn't stop. I felt like a character in a book. The whole class just sat there, until finally Henry called Miss Gohagan. She had been talking to Kathy Harrell in the hall, but she hurried in and led me out and closed the door. Then she put her arm around my shoulders and walked me up and down until I was calm. I spent the rest of the afternoon lying on the cot in the nurse's office.

CHAPTER 26

I was looking through the morning paper for an interesting current event to put in my journal. That's when I saw this headline: SEVEN SISTERS FREEWAY BLASTING SCHEDULED. I tried to read the whole article all at once, which was kind of like trying to cram a whole slice of pizza in my mouth.

> Blasting begins tomorrow at 6:00 A.M. on the pass through the foothills . . . making way for the new six-lane highway . . . The Seven Sisters Freeway will allow easy access to Windsor for residents of the foothills communities of Mountain Meadows, Spring Valley, and Windsor Forest. Construction in these communities has been growing steadily for months, and the freeway is expected to further contribute to that area's building boom. . . . slated for completion by mid-1973.

"Don't scream in the house, sweetheart," Dad said. "Whatta ya got there?" He looked over my shoulder. "Oh, yeah. It's that new highway to White Heaven, better known as Mountain Meadows. Nothing but fake mansions as far as the eye can see."

"They're going to dynamite the *mountains?*" I said.

"Well, no, not exactly. See, they're gonna dynamite a pass through the hills. The homes aren't being built on the Seven Sisters—they're in the area between Windsor and the Sisters. There's a lot of new construction out that way. People are trying to get away from the city."

"How can they go and do stuff like this?" I asked. "Do they think it doesn't matter? They think they can do anything they want, and if a mountain's in the way, well, they'll just blow it up!"

"Lots of taxpayers in those new neighborhoods," Dad said. "Money talks. Besides, we're not talking about sensible people, here. These are mostly folks who are scared to death a black family might move next door."

I couldn't believe what I was hearing. "They'd rather *blow up* a mountain than live near black people?" I asked.

"Yeah. Go figure."

"Will we be able to see it, or hear it?"

"Maybe hear it, if the wind's blowing in our direction," Dad said.

I didn't know if the wind was blowing in our direction or not, but I went outside early the next morning. I got up the minute I heard Dad's alarm go off. I was wearing flannel pajamas, and I threw my ski jacket on over them and pulled on my boots. The Secret Garden was nearly invisible, but I sat on my chunk of firewood and waited. My feet were flat on the ground in front of me. Maybe I would feel the earth shake when the dynamite went off.

I sat there for what seemed like a long time. I never felt anything, or heard anything, and I finally went inside to get my bath and get ready for school.

At my piano lesson that afternoon, Mrs. Gandy noticed that I wasn't in a very good mood. "You're not playing very happy, Amanda," she said.

"No." How could I play happy on a day like that, especially when my piano lesson began with me waiting in the hall while Vanessa took her time? She was like a thorn in my side. I couldn't even look at her without getting mad.

Mrs. Gandy looked at me a few seconds, and then she played some chords on the piano that sounded even sadder than Sporty's singing. I couldn't believe it.

"Mrs. Gandy," I said, "do *you* play the blues, too?"

She closed her eyes and played, and it was like she had forgotten that I was even there. It made me want to shake her arm, to bring her back.

When she stopped playing, I sat there and looked at her. "Do you sometimes feel like that inside?" I asked.

"Yes, sometimes I do."

That was something to think about.

"Sometimes Sporty does, too," I said. "Have you ever heard him sing the blues?"

"Yes, I've heard him," she said. "Albert can make that guitar of his talk, and he can make it weep, too."

"Henry Bailey said that Sporty has had trouble in his life."

"That he has. Albert had a son in Vietnam who never did make it back home. It's been three years ago, and they say they don't know if he's dead, or a prisoner of war, or what. Missing in Action, that's what they say."

We didn't talk about it anymore, but I never forgot the way Mrs. Gandy played the piano that day. One thing was for sure: She had had trouble in her life, too.

On the bus ride home, I kept hearing Mrs. Gandy's blues in my head. The blues sounded the way I'd felt when I heard about the dynamiting near the Seven Sisters, and when I found out I'd be going to school without Jackie. Missing Jackie was the worst, though. I would get used to the hill being gone when we drove to Sapphire Mountain, but I would never get used to Jackie being blasted out of my life. Blasted out of my life by busing, I thought. Ha. I had the busing blues. For the rest of the ride home I stared out the window and made up words to my own personal blues song.

> *Let me off this school bus,*
> *Just let me off, I say.*
> *This danged old rackety school bus*
> *Takes me miles out of my way.*
> *Just want to go home.*
> *I got the busing blues.*

I guess my blues song wasn't *real* blues, though, because making it up made me feel better.

Our class had a Halloween party on the Friday before Halloween, and our church Halloween party was Saturday night.

160

I was a bum, so I wore an old pair of Dad's pants tied around my waist with a piece of twine, and an old sport coat we'd found at the PTA Thrift Store. Mom drew some stubble on my face, and I stuffed my hair under an old hat that Dad had worn back in the fifties.

I felt okay about my costume until I saw Jackie's. She was dressed like a flapper, in a fringed yellow dress with a matching band around her head that had a feather attached to one side. She had on red lipstick and wore a long string of beads, and I had to admit she looked great. She said hi, but that was it. She talked a lot to Heather Baker, who went to New Canaan Academy. I went over and talked to Jennifer.

"I like your costume," Jennifer said, "but what happened to the Siamese twins?"

"We got surgically separated," I said. "The operation was a complete success."

Jennifer was dressed as a clown, but her white clown makeup didn't quite hide her freckles. "Where'd you get the cool wig?" I asked. She wore a short white wig, and the hair had been teased so that it stood straight up.

"It was my grandmother's," she said, and her big red clown grin got even bigger. "It made her head itch, so she never wore it. Now it's making my head itch. I've got a floppy red hat with white polka dots on it around here somewhere, but wearing it on top made the itching even worse."

"It looks great," I said. "Save me a seat near you when it's time for refreshments, okay? I've got to go play the piano."

Miss Elaine had asked me to play some songs on the piano in the fellowship hall, and I had tried to find some good ones. I opened my briefcase and set it beside the piano so I could get to my sheet music. First I played "My Grandfather's Clock," of course, and then I did some other easy, fun little songs that I thought everybody would like. I felt pretty good.

Then a real miracle happened, right there in the church fellowship hall (which I guess is a good place for a miracle). Jackie sat down next to me at the piano and said, "Follow the Leader! Let's play our duet."

"Okay." I held up one hand to count the beat, and said, "Ah one, ah two, ah one two three four," and we launched into "Heart and Soul" like we had never had an argument. We flubbed up, but it was good and loud, and I used all the advice that Mrs. Gandy had given me about playing.

Afterward, Jackie bowed about twenty times, like she was the star of the show. Then she stood on the piano bench and shook her fringe until Miss Elaine made her get down.

I went to get a chocolate cupcake with orange icing and candy corn on top. I was ladling orange punch into a plastic cup when Jennifer came over. She already had her plate and punch. "Still want me to save you a seat?" she asked. I guessed that she had seen me talking to Jackie.

"Yes!" I said. "I'll be right there." I didn't want Jackie to start being my friend again because she felt sorry for me. It reminded me of the dumb joke about tying a pork chop around a little boy's neck so the dog will play with him. I wasn't *that* bad.

I sat next to Jennifer at one of the long folding tables that my church uses for everything. Sometimes they were decorated for weddings or baby showers, and sometimes they were plain, like for potluck dinners, but they were always the same old tables. It gave me a good feeling to know that some things never changed.

Once everybody stopped paying attention to her, Jackie came over and sat across from me. She smiled.

It was a scary smile, because Jackie had put a fake mole near the left corner of her mouth, like Marilyn Monroe. She said, "Why don't you come over to my house tomorrow and we'll play Aggravation?"

Her eyes were shining like a jack-o-lantern's. I looked at her, and I knew in a flash that I didn't want to go to Jackie's house and play Aggravation, or talk about clothes, or hear about who was doing what at her stupid private school.

"I'll ask my mom," I told her. "But I don't think she'll let me."

Jackie stopped smiling. But she didn't look hurt. She looked mad.

"I guess you've got so many nigger friends now that you don't need me," she said. "I hope your new friends don't kill you when they start to riot."

Jennifer's mouth dropped open, and she set her cupcake down on her plate.

"Why would they?" I asked. "They know me and Jennifer, and they like us. They'd be more likely to come after *you,* and all the other little snots who think they're too good to go to school with black people."

"I'll be so sorry to hear that you died in a fire at that school. I'll cry at your funeral when your boyfriend Henry beats you to death and throws your body in a ditch."

I slapped my hand down on the fellowship hall folding

table. The whole room got quiet. I remember seeing Jennifer's little brother, Jamie. He had been bobbing for apples, and when I slapped the table his head came up out of the bucket with water dripping off his cheeks and ears.

"You better shut your ugly mouth," I said. I didn't yell at all. I said it calmly and quietly. "I'm sick of your comments. And I'll tell you something else—I'm sick of YOU . . . *Beastle.*"

I didn't know I was going to say that. I felt the same way I'd felt the day I slapped her. Jackie looked like she'd been slapped, too. She opened her mouth, but nothing came out.

Miss Elaine put her hand on my shoulder. "Girls," she said, "if you can't get along, I'm going to have to separate you. Jackie, you go to that side of the room, and Amanda, you stay right here. I've a good mind to call your mothers. . . ."

Well, in my opinion, Miss Elaine *didn't* have a good mind, but in the end she did call our mothers. She said that we were spoiling the party for the smaller children. That was really Jackie's fault, because she sat on her side of the room and kept talking about me loud enough so I'd be sure to hear it. Jennifer sat with me to show her support even though she could have been playing games.

My mom got to the church first, which made it sort of like I had won. "What's the matter with you, Amanda?" she asked as we went out to the car. "Is it really necessary for me to have to pick you up from a church party for *fighting*?"

"I guess so," I said. "When Jackie keeps making prejudiced remarks." I slid into the front seat and sat with my head against the cool glass of the car window, looking at the stars and at my reflection in the window.

"Maybe your dad's right," Mom said. "Maybe we should try to find another church, where more people think the way we do about desegregation." I could feel her looking at me.

"Okay," I said. I didn't move my head away from the window. I could see the reflection of the right side of my face, and I looked mysterious and (in my opinion) almost pretty, even wearing fake stubble. Then I looked at her. "No, I don't want to change churches," I said. "I have to stick with Jennifer Reddenfield. If I leave, she'll be the only normal person left."

I don't know if it was the cupcake, or the orange punch that Miss Elaine had made. Whatever it was, that night I had a weird dream. I dreamed Jackie and I were friends. She was smiling and saying, "Come on over to my house." But I wouldn't go with her. Instead, I ran to the top of a mountain, and when I got to the top I wasn't tired at all. A cool wind blew my hair back, and my hair had grown longer than Laura's. It blew my clothes, too. I wore a poncho, and all that empty cloth flapped around me in the breeze.

CHAPTER 27

The next Friday we finished reading *Huckleberry Finn.* The last couple of chapters were exciting, but our whole class got mad at Tom Sawyer for acting the way he did. He had known all along that Jim wasn't a slave anymore because his owner had died and set him free in her will, but he didn't tell Jim and Huck. Instead, he pretended like he was helping Jim escape.

"That was *wrong,*" Gaylyn Graves said. "He's acting like it's all a big game, but it was Jim's *life.* And he could have got him killed, acting like he did and letting everybody else think Jim was a runaway slave."

Kyle said, "All that stuff he made Jim do, and there was no reason for it." His face was red. "It was like torture, what he did, and all because he wanted to have an adventure!"

"He is one sick little old boy," Joenathan said, shaking his head. "I mean, that is sick, to do somebody that way."

Nobody was madder at Tom Sawyer than Henry Bailey. "Somebody ought to chain him up, see how *he* likes it!" he said.

* * *

Some days were still nice enough for us to have recess outside, and whenever we went out Henry made me practice our boost. We pretty much had it down to a science, and Henry was dying to try it on the Wall again. But we never seemed to get a chance. I think Miss Gohagan was still afraid that our class couldn't work together as a team. We would probably never get out of Phase I of her red booklet. Then I wondered: What would Phase II be? "Busing Pajama Parties?" Ha.

"Miss Gohagan!" Henry said. "I'm ready to try that Wall again now."

Miss Gohagan just said, "Henry, if you had applied yourself to your schoolwork last year with the same energy you've expended toward that Wall, you would never have had to repeat sixth grade."

Henry Bailey walked along beside Miss Gohagan. He put his hand up on her shoulder as we all walked back toward the school. "I'm *liking* the sixth grade this year. I might just do this again next year! What you say, Miss G.? Can I be in your class again next year?"

"No, Henry, if you fail sixth grade again, you'll go to a different teacher. You'd be in Mr. Gordon's class."

Henry removed his hand like he'd been burned. "Say what? I am *not* going in Commander Gordon's class. I'll *pass* the sixth grade this time, Miss G. You just gave me my incentive."

"Excellent use of vocabulary, Henry," Miss Gohagan said.

"You know me, Miss G.—I don't play."

I walked with Amy Voorhees back to class. I had made an

early New Year's resolution: I was going to get a new best friend. I would be outgoing and cheerful and helpful, and I would find *somebody*! I decided Amy would make an excellent best friend.

"Henry's crazy," I said, as a conversation starter.

"He sure is," she said.

"I think he's really worked out a way to get us all over that Wall, though. I hope we get a chance to do it before the end of the year."

Amy didn't seem too interested in that, so I got right to the point. "Listen, Amy, my mom says I can have a friend over this weekend. Do you want to ride home on the bus with me Friday, and spend the night? We can make chocolate chip cookies, and play records and stuff."

"I'll have to check with Mama," Amy said. "But I probably can."

"Great! You can bring your stuff to school, and my dad will take you home Saturday afternoon. Here's my phone number, in case your mom wants to call my mom first."

Making friends was easy. All it took was a little self-confidence. I went through the rest of the day feeling very self-confident. That's why I decided to volunteer for the *Huckleberry Finn* project.

Since we had finished reading *Huckleberry Finn,* Miss Gohagan had a surprise. "We're going to share parts of *Huckleberry Finn* with the fifth-graders," she said. "We'll have two or three groups of students from this class perform a dramatic reading. We'll select a scene from the book that we think the younger students will enjoy, and the groups will go from classroom to classroom."

When Miss Gohagan asked who would be interested in performing, my hand went up.

We would perform two different scenes. I was going to be the narrator of the scene where Huck tells Jim about kings, and then he tries to explain that kings from France speak French, instead of English. Jim doesn't understand that at all. It was one of the funniest scenes in the book.

Miss Gohagan wrote out the parts. I only had a little bit to read at the beginning, and then David (playing Jim) and Kyle (playing Huck) talked back and forth. David and Kyle had become friends. Sometimes Kyle stood with David and sort of unofficially helped him be hall monitor. They were really excited about working together on their scene.

"We're not going to use the dialects that Mark Twain wrote," Miss Gohagan said. "I want you to pronounce the words the way we normally do." Dialect, she had told us, was when you wrote down the words and spelled them the way they sounded when people talked.

"For instance, people from the Northeast part of the United States would think that *we* all sound funny," Miss Gohagan had said. That was true; Dad was constantly making fun of the way Mom talked.

My group did a rehearsal of our scene, and another group (Kathy, Darlene, Gaylyn, and Joenathan) did theirs. We rehearsed in front of the rest of the class, and they were supposed to give us their opinion on how we did. As soon as our scene was done, Miss Gohagan asked for comments. Victoria Moore's hand shot up.

"Miss Gohagan!" she said. "I have a comment." She was quiet for a little while and sat with her head tilted toward her shoulder as she thought about what she planned to say. "I don't like that scene," she said. "It makes Jim sound like he's stupid."

Miss Gohagan nodded slowly. "*Huck Finn* is a complicated book," she said. "I almost decided against reading it this year, because of some of the problems it raises. But remember that Mark Twain wrote this book almost ninety years ago. Attitudes have changed a tremendous amount since then. You can read *Huckleberry Finn* and tell yourself, 'This book makes black people seem ignorant and superstitious at times, and I don't like that.' But the fundamental truth of the book, as I see it, is that Huck Finn himself, an ignorant, superstitious white boy, comes to realize that a black man is a human being. He laughs at Jim, and sometimes he treats Jim like a child, but even with his attitudes and prejudices and wrongheadedness, being with Jim and living with him day to day forces him to realize that Jim is a person. Do you see what I mean? I think the truth of that is more important than anything else. There's a lot we can learn from Huck and Jim, about how we need each other, and how we should treat each other. But you're right, Victoria. Now that we've taken this scene out of the book, we can see more clearly how Jim is treated. Let's pick a different scene to portray. Who has a suggestion?"

* * *

I had everything ready for Amy Voorhees to come spend the night at my house. I asked Mom to make lasagna for dinner. I made Dad promise not to tease Amy until *after* supper, after she'd had a chance to get used to him. I knew Laura would be fine, so I didn't have to ask her to do anything special. When the last bell rang on Friday afternoon, I caught up with Amy in the hallway. "I'm on bus one-twelve," I told her. "If we hurry, we can get a seat in the very back." I didn't like sitting in the back of the bus by myself, but with a friend to talk to and laugh with, it was fun.

Amy's eyes got huge and her mouth dropped open. "Oh, no!" she said. "I completely forgot, Amanda."

"You forgot you were going home with me?" I asked. I stopped in the hall, and an ocean of kids washed past.

"I forgot to tell Mama," Amy said. "I completely forgot, and the last thing she said to me this morning was that she was going to pick me up, because we're going to visit my grandma for the weekend. I'm so sorry, Amanda. I'm really, really, sorry."

"It's okay," I said. I could tell Amy felt awful about it, and I didn't want to make her feel any worse. I faked a sneeze, so that maybe she'd think my eyes were watering from a cold or something. "We'll do it another time."

Once I got home and talked to Mom about it, I didn't feel as bad about my messed-up weekend with Amy. Mom said we could move it to the next weekend if Amy could come then. I thought everything would be fine, until Monday afternoon when I heard Amy talking to Kathy in the hall.

I was walking toward the front of the school, but instead of going out the front door, I was going to take a left turn and head down the steps to the music room. Amy and Kathy were standing right there at the top of the steps, and they didn't see me coming.

I turned the corner and heard Amy say, "I thought she was going to *cry*. . . ."

As soon as they saw me, and I saw the looks on their faces, I knew they had been talking about me. Amy was telling the whole world how desperate I was to have a friend.

I went past them without saying anything and sat in the art room to wait for Vanessa to leave. I didn't turn the lights on. It felt better to sit in the dark. Nothing was worse than knowing that people were talking about me behind my back. And since Amy and Kathy knew I'd heard them talking about me, they would think I was mad and would avoid me. I would have loved it if I could have done that to *them,* but I didn't have many friends at EWE. If Amy and Kathy stopped talking to me, I was doomed.

I heard Mrs. Gandy's door open, and I waited until Vanessa had gone upstairs. I felt better as soon as I was with Mrs. Gandy. She and I talked for a minute, and then I got ready to play "Jesu, Joy of Man's Desiring." I had been working on it a lot, and I wanted to impress Mrs. Gandy with how much better I was. But once I started playing, I made the same mistake I always made.

"I'm going to start over," I said, waving my hands in the

air like I could erase the wrong notes. But Mrs. Gandy was shaking her head.

"The piece is moving *on,* whether you're playing it or not. It's in the air all the time. You deciding to play it is just like jumping in a river for a swim. You have to keep going on downstream." Her piano music went merrily downstream.

"Like Huck Finn and Jim going down the Mississippi on the raft," I said. "But what if the current pulls me under and I drown?"

"Child, what kind of talk is that? If you feel like you're getting in too deep, you just jerk your hands up, so! And you go back to the baby pool until you've built up your muscles."

"Maybe I just better go back to the baby pool, then," I said, sadly.

"Two things," Mrs. Gandy said, rolling her stool away from the piano. "First: there is no shame in this world in going back to the baby pool. That's where you build your skill. And I don't care what it is you do with your life, there's gonna be times you got to go backward before you can move ahead. Second: This is not one of those times. You can play this piece. You can play this piece just like Mr. Bach intended for it to be played. You are just letting yourself fret too much over it." She grabbed my shoulders and swayed me back and forth. I laughed, letting my head roll on my neck. "There you go," Mrs. Gandy said. "Now get down there and play!"

We went over the song a couple of times, and Mrs. Gandy gave me some advice on how to handle the hard parts. We were talking and laughing, and I felt so much better than when I'd first walked in.

Somebody knocked at the classroom door.

"Come in!" Mrs. Gandy said. She looked surprised.

It was Vanessa. "Mrs. Gandy?" she said. "Can I ask you a question?"

"Of course you can. Come on in here—Amanda and I were just finishing up." She turned back to me. "Amanda, you're making good progress. You work on that some more, and I'll see you next Monday."

I think I said good-bye before I left, but I don't really know. I was so mad at Vanessa that I wanted to cry, and scream, and throw things. I walked down the hallway past Sporty's office, which was empty this afternoon, and started climbing the stairs to the first floor. My feet felt like they were being held to the floor with strong magnets. It was hard to get my knees to work. I don't know what was wrong with me, but I suddenly felt like Vanessa was the Beastle. The hateful, foul-breathed Beastle that had come between me and Jackie and split us apart forever. The Beastle that poisoned the air and kept me from making a new friend.

I heard Vanessa as she ran down the hall behind me. "Good-bye, Mrs. Gandy!" she called over her shoulder.

I had stopped on the stairs, and when Vanessa came running up them she wasn't looking, and she ran right into my briefcase. She hit it so hard she nearly knocked it out of my hand, and I stumbled on the steps and hit my hip against the handrail. I felt tears in my eyes. I don't know if they came when I hurt my hip, or if they were already there.

"I'm sorry!" Vanessa said. Her eyes were wide, like she knew she was in trouble. She held out her hand like she could straighten up my briefcase and make everything all right again.

I slapped her hand away. My teeth gritted together. I wanted to explode. I looked at Vanessa and said the worst thing I could think of.

"Get away from me, you stupid nigger."

Vanessa ran up the steps and out the front door. I rubbed my sore hip and closed my eyes to keep the tears from coming out.

"Amanda Adams." I had never heard that tone in Mrs. Gandy's voice before. I turned, and Mrs. Gandy was standing at the bottom of the steps.

I wondered if it would be possible to die from shame. I stared down at the shiny dark brown floor tiles in the hallway. I knew I couldn't say anything without crying.

So I turned and ran.

"What's the matter?" Mom asked when I got in the car.

"I had a bad day," I said. "I don't want to talk about it."

I hated that school. I never wanted to go near it again. And I never wanted to see Mrs. Gandy again, not for as long as I lived.

CHAPTER 28

On my next piano lesson day I told Mom I was sick. It was my first absence of the year. School had been awful all week, with me trying not to run into Mrs. Gandy anywhere and trying to act cool around Kathy and Amy. Over the weekend all I could think about was how I wouldn't be able to face Mrs. Gandy on Monday afternoon. By the time I went to bed Sunday night, I really did feel terrible. When Mom called me Monday morning, I told her I was too sick to go to school.

She came into my room and put her hand on my forehead. "You don't have a fever," she said skeptically.

"I can't help it if I don't have a fever," I said. "I feel sick!" I started crying.

"All right," Mom said. Her voice was soft and calm, and she rubbed the back of her hand against my cheek. "Can I get you anything?"

"I want my bumbie," I said. Mom gave me a funny look, but she got my bee-sting blanket and put it on top of my other covers. She brought me a glass of ginger ale, too. Ted jumped on my bed and started rooting around on the bee-sting blanket. He liked it as much as I did.

"Is it your stomach, Amanda?" Mom asked. "Or do you hurt somewhere else?"

"I don't know. I guess it's my stomach." I couldn't tell her that Mrs. Gandy had looked right down to the bottom of me and had seen exactly what kind of person I really was. She saw that when I wasn't afraid of being beaten up, I had no principles at all. She saw that I was one of those people you heard about in church, the kind who pretended to be good when they weren't: a *hypocrite*.

I couldn't tell Mom what I'd done, either. I had to live with it stuck inside me forever, because I didn't want anybody else to see what I was really like. Mom could tell there was something going on, and she kept trying to get me to talk about it. I finally told her about Amy and Kathy talking about me in the hall, and that made me start crying again.

Mom held me tight, bumbie and all. "I'm so proud of you," she whispered. "I know it's been a difficult school year, with all the changes you've faced. And you've faced them like a soldier, Amanda. You're a whole lot tougher than you think you are. Be tough a little while longer, and soon you'll see that things aren't as terrible as they seem to you right now. I promise."

When Mom left, I rolled over with the covers pulled all the way up to my nose and lay there like a lump. Mom wouldn't have been proud of me if she'd known what I'd done. I stared out my bedroom window. I could see a piece of the backyard, and nothing else. I looked out the window and pretended like I was lying in the loft of the cabin on Sapphire Mountain and the world was falling away from me, leaving me at the very top. And the way I imagined it, it was summer, and all the flowers were foaming up and washing the sky clean. I thought if I could breathe in that flower-scrubbed air, maybe I could be clean, too.

I slept until almost suppertime. When I got up, I wrapped my bumbie around me and went into the den. Laura was sitting in there, reading.

"Hey, Little Bit," she said. "I was about to come get you. It's impossible to concentrate when there's nobody in there banging on the piano. Go play something for me."

I flopped onto the couch with my knees hanging over the arm. "I can't," I said.

Miss Gohagan welcomed me back to school the next day like I had been gone for weeks. "I'm particularly glad that everyone is here today," she said, "because we have a special guest coming to visit this afternoon."

After lunch Miss Gohagan introduced the visitor. "Mr. Arlen Randolph has come here today to talk to us about poetry," she said. "Some of you may have read Mr. Randolph's column in the newspaper. If you haven't, I want you to start looking for it this week. It has his picture right beside it. Now that you know what Mr. Randolph looks like, that should make it easy to find."

Mr. Randolph smiled at the class and said, "But it *is* a lousy picture." He was a tall black man with short gray hair. He wore little half glasses on the end of his nose.

Miss Gohagan went on. "Mr. Randolph was born in Virginia, attended Wilmont College, and received his master's degree in English from the University of North Carolina. He has published books about poets and poetry, as well as on other topics. Please give him your attention—we are very fortunate to have him visit with us."

Miss Gohagan pulled her chair over beside the window and sat down.

Mr. Randolph stood up and walked in front of Miss Gohagan's desk. He sat on the edge of the desk and propped a thin book on his right leg. He had the longest fingers I'd ever seen. "It's a pleasure to be with you today," he said. He had a deep voice, smoother than the bass keys on the piano.

I followed the rhythms of his voice as he talked about when he was in school, and about his favorite books. He talked about poetry, and then he read us a poem by a poet named John Crowe Ransom, called "Bells for John Whiteside's Daughter." It was sad, but beautiful.

Then Mr. Randolph read some more poems. It made me understand how a piano must feel when somebody has been playing a sad, lonesome song on it, and then they change and start playing something that makes you want to dance.

"This will be the last poem I read," Mr. Randolph said, flipping through his book. It's by Langston Hughes, and the title of the poem is 'Dream Variations.' "

> *To fling my arms wide*
> *In some place of the sun,*
> *To whirl and to dance*
> *Till the white day is done.*
> *Then rest at cool evening*

Beneath a tall tree
While night comes on gently,
 Dark like me—
That is my dream!

To fling my arms wide
In the face of the sun,
Dance! Whirl! Whirl!
Till the quick day is done.
Rest at pale evening . . .
A tall, slim tree . . .
Night coming tenderly
 Black like me.

I was surprised, because I'd never heard a poem about being black before. I wondered if Henry liked that poem, but when I turned just enough to see him, he was sitting slouched down in his seat with his eyes closed. Typical Henry.

Mr. Randolph closed the book gently. He looked up and smiled. "I'll leave you to think about these poems," he said. "Thank you for inviting me to visit your class." And with that, he walked out.

As the door closed behind Mr. Randolph, Marcella said, "Miss Gohagan, let's write a paper about those poems!"

Henry sat straight up. "Shut up!" he said, and everybody laughed.

"Henry, please," Miss Gohagan said. "Each one of us will write a thank-you note to Mr. Randolph for coming and speaking to us today. And I can drop them off at the paper after school."

She stood up and passed out thick, creamy paper to each row. It was much nicer than the kind of paper the school usually provided.

"If you would like to tell Mr. Randolph how the poems made you feel, I think that would be wonderful," Miss Gohagan said.

I wrote that "Bells for John Whiteside's Daughter" was my favorite poem, even though it was sad. "It makes you want to cry," I wrote, "but you don't ever want to stop hearing it."

I turned my letter facedown on my desk and felt Henry's sharp finger in my back. "Here, Amanda Adams," he said. He tossed his letter over my shoulder. Henry had written, "Thank you for coming to our class and killing an hour. Henry T. Bailey."

"Everyone finish up now," Miss Gohagan said, "and pass your letters to the front of the row."

Papers rustled forward, and soon I had five letters on my desk—everybody's except Marcella's. I turned to look, but she was still bent over her paper, writing on the back of the page.

Henry saw me looking, and he turned around, too. "Beastle, would you please sign your Beastley name and go *on*? Everybody is waiting on you."

She acted like she hadn't heard him. She wrote a couple more words, then looked up. Her eyes were shining, and her bangs were all messed up from where she'd been running her hands through them.

"Here," she said, holding out her paper, but she jerked it back when Henry reached for it. "Not you!" she said, and she leaned forward to hand the paper to me.

I placed it facedown on the top of the stack of letters, and I couldn't help but read what was written on the back. Marcella had written a poem!

You see that balloon?
Joy makes it rise—
Sends it up into the skies.
See that fountain of water spray?
That's joy *that makes it do that way.*
That's joy that makes my heart just sing.
Why, joy's the best of everything.

She had signed her letter, "Your friend, Joy Bailey."

I added her letter to the stack as Miss Gohagan reached our row.

"Thank you," Miss Gohagan said. She placed all the letters on her desk. "Now, let's get out our math workbooks."

I reached down to pull my workbook out of my desk and turned my head to look behind Henry. "Great poem," I whispered to her.

She frowned and leaned forward. "What?" she said.

Henry leaned over and put his face between us. I tried to stare him down, but he just stared back.

This time I talked loud enough for her to hear me.

"Great poem, Joy," I said.

CHAPTER 29

Two days later, right before our first class field trip, Miss Gohagan passed out copies of Arlen Randolph's latest newspaper column. He had written the whole column about visiting the sixth-grade classes at EWE, and he printed parts of some of the thank-you letters he got. He finished his column by printing Joy's poem! I tore a corner off one page of my math workbook and wrote Joy a note:

Dear Joy, I told you your poem was great! Aren't you happy it got printed in the newspaper?

Then I got in trouble for passing notes.

Our field trip was to Bethabra, a place where Moravian settlers had come and started a town. Even though Windsor had turned into a city around it, everything there was still like olden times. I had gone there on a field trip every year since third grade.

On the bus, I found a seat near the back and slid over to the window. Spaghetti Eddie was coming down the sidewalk, with his stiff brown hat pulled way down over his eyes. Henry saw him, too. He jumped into the seat beside me and leaned over to pull the window down. I got a view of Henry's belly button as his arms went up to lower the window. I poked him in the belly. He doubled over, but it didn't distract him.

"Spaghetti Eddie!" Henry yelled. "Hey—Spaghetti Eddie, with the meatball eyes! Ya mamma gonna leave you when ya daddy dies!"

He laughed like a maniac when Spaghetti Eddie whirled around and cursed him.

"I loves that Spaghetti Eddie," Henry said to himself as he jerked the window back up.

"Get out of there, Henry Bailey, and stop bothering Amanda," Joy said. She pulled him out of the way and sat next to me.

"Beastle, I ain't bothering nobody but that ugly old Spaghetti Eddie. Don't you be laying your Beastley hands on me. Hey! There's Sporty Deane."

Sporty was walking toward our bus, and when he saw Spaghetti Eddie, he stopped and said something to him. Then Sporty got on the bus. He stood at the front and said, "Miss Gohagan asked me to come along and help keep you all straight. So I better not see any cuttin' up or carryin' on." He smiled when he said it, though.

"Hey, Sporty!" Henry yelled. "Come sit back here! I'm saving you a seat."

Sporty sat with Henry in the seat in front of us. "Yes, you exactly the one I need to watch the closest."

"What you talking to that old Spaghetti Eddie for, anyway?" Henry asked. "Ain't you afraid you might catch something?" Henry pointed down the sidewalk, where Spaghetti Eddie was leaning against the fence, watching traffic go by. He had his back to us.

Sporty leaned forward to look out the window where Henry was pointing; then he sat back. "Lay off my man, there, Henry. Don't you know who that is?"

"Yeah," Henry said, smart as ever, "it's the ugliest man in Smoketown. Wears the ugliest suit and hat, too."

"No, sir. That's Guitar Gabriel Moore. He's the hottest blues man this side of Memphis, Tennessee. Did an album a couple of years back. Don't you be giving Guitar Gabriel any trouble. He don't look like much on the outside, but inside he's full of soul."

"Say he's called Guitar Gabriel?" Henry asked.

"That's right. One day he's going to make another album, too, and guess who's going to play backup for him? Me. That's what I can't wait for. Guitar Gabriel going to make a comeback."

The bus pulled onto the highway, and the noise made it hard to hear anything else that Sporty and Henry said. I looked at Joy, and she smiled.

"I really liked your poem," I told her.

Her smile got two times bigger. My dad would say she had a one-hundred-watt smile. "Listening to those poems he read just set me off," she said. "Sometimes I see something, or hear something, and it's like the rest of the world isn't even there anymore." She was quiet a minute, and then she said, "One day I was working in my history book, and I looked down, and one of my eyelashes had fallen onto the page. It looked just like a parenthesis where it fell. That's the kind of thing that makes me want to write a poem."

I thought about the pictures I used to see in *Highlights* magazine when I was waiting at the dentist's office. The pictures had things hidden in them, and you were supposed to see how many of them you could find. There might be a wheelbarrow hidden in the branches of a tree, or a rabbit in the clouds. It seemed to me that Joy would be really good at finding all that hidden stuff.

I walked around Bethabra with her. Joy had been there before, too, but it was fun seeing it again. The biggest building there was called the Single Brothers' House, where unmarried men lived. They did things like woodworking, and they ran a school for boys in the house. We walked down the block to the Moravian bakery, where we got free samples of crisp ginger cookies, and we stopped at the house where the town doctor had lived.

It was a big day for class trips at Bethabra. Everywhere we went, we passed other groups of kids, but the tour guides had fixed it so that none of us would be in exactly the same place at the same time. We went through the museum behind a group of little third-graders, but we lost them when we stopped to watch a group of women who were busy weaving cloth and making hand-dipped beeswax candles.

"I love to smell those candles," Joy said. "I can just smell the honeybees in them."

The Moravian church and cemetery were the last things we saw before we got back on the bus. The cemetery was plain, with flat white headstones. Our guide explained that families weren't buried together. Instead, people were buried in what they called choirs—single women were together in one choir, single men in another, married women in another, et cetera.

"But why would they go to all that trouble?" I asked Joy. "They're dead—they're not going to care who they're buried next to."

Sporty heard me. "It's the ones still living that care," he said.

As we walked away from the cemetery, we passed a small group of kids about our age going in the opposite direction. One girl in the group was talking really loud, and the teacher kept saying, "Now, let's not disturb everyone else today, please. Keep your voices at a reasonable level."

I recognized that voice right away. It was Jackie, with her classmates from New Canaan Academy. She never saw me. I didn't try to avoid her on purpose—I wasn't ashamed to be seen walking with Joy. The thing is, I wanted to watch Jackie and pretend like we were total strangers. That way, I thought maybe I could tell what she was really like. All I saw was a loudmouthed, cute girl in a green jacket who kept making her friends laugh. I didn't see a hateful, prejudiced person. But I knew that's what she was.

Then I had a sort of new idea. At least it was new to me, and it really did feel like a lightbulb switched on in my head. The idea was this: In one way, Jackie was no different from me. We were both scared of people who were different from us, and we didn't like feeling scared. But I had gotten the chance to get to know some of the different people, and

Jackie hadn't. At first the black kids in my class had seemed like a scary group of strangers. Now they were just Henry and Joenathan and David and Joy and Victoria and Gaylyn.

Joy and I sat together on the bus to go back to school, too, but we didn't talk much. I did ask her, though, "Joy, were you sort of scared when you found out that a bunch of white kids were coming to your school this year?"

"*No,*" she said, and she smiled as she shook her head. "I got so excited! I thought it would be like the preachers say Heaven is—everybody all together like a family reunion, and nobody remembering anything bad that ever happened in the past."

I thought that she must have been really disappointed. "Did it turn out like that?" I asked finally.

"It will get to be like that, someday," she said. She sounded pretty sure of herself. "I wrote a poem about it, and the end of it goes: 'Someday the clouds won't hide the sun, and the rays will shine on everyone.' "

I turned to look out the bus window. The glass was cold, and I leaned my forehead against it.

I imagined myself as an adult, with long flowing blond hair. I would be a famous conductor, and I would be able to tell people, "Joy Bailey, the poet? Oh, yes, we were in school together."

Everyone would be amazed that two such great people had come from Windsor, North Carolina.

My group performed our scene from *Huckleberry Finn* all day on Friday, going around to different fifth-grade classes.

We had decided to do part of the scene where Huck dresses up like a girl. He disguised himself so he could find out what people in town think happened to him. I played Mrs. Judith Loftus, Kyle was Huck, and David was the narrator. By the third time we did it, we had gotten pretty good, and the little kids laughed at all the right places. I even saw Vanessa laughing when we did the scene for her class, and she clapped with everybody else when it was over. As we left, I passed her desk. "I'm sorry about what I said," I whispered to her. She didn't say anything back. She looked at me with her big dark eyes, then smiled real big at David.

Mom had been right. It took less than two weeks for things at school to get better. Kathy had smiled at me, and kept asking me questions like what was I reading, and where did I get my new smock top. Amy was still acting kind of funny, but I guessed that she felt more ashamed of herself than anything else. I knew that pretty soon she would come up and say something to me, and we'd both act like nothing had happened. That's how girls apologized to each other, most of the time.

Now I only had one problem left: Mrs. Gandy. She wasn't another girl, and I knew that I had to *do* something to make things right with her. I thought about it all weekend, knowing that on Monday afternoon I'd have to be ready to face her again. I couldn't stop thinking about it, but I couldn't come up with any good ideas, either. I thought that maybe if I paid better attention in church, I would be rewarded by hearing the perfect answer. Church was supposed to help, after all. So I listened to the sermon, which was based on I Corinthians 13:9–12. Verse 12 was the one that got my attention. "For now we see in a mirror dimly, but then face to face. Now I know in part; then I shall understand fully, even as I have been fully understood."

I couldn't stop thinking about that verse. It made me think again about the idea of looking in a mirror and seeing a backward reflection. Was that what that verse was talking about? Not being able to see what I was really like, because my reflection was backward? Then, when I got to Heaven I'd be able to see exactly what was wrong with me and fix it. Well, it sort of made sense, but I still didn't see how it could help me fix things with Mrs. Gandy, now.

"Amanda, wake up," Mom said, shaking my elbow. "We're going to have lunch at the K & W Cafeteria, and we'd like to beat the rush."

By Monday morning, I still didn't have any magic solution to my problem. Finally, while I was supposed to be reading a page in my science book about how people predict the weather, I wrote this note:

Dear Mrs. Gandy:
I want to tell you that you are my favorite teacher I've ever had in six years of school, and maybe after I've been in school another six or ten years I'll be smart enough not to say stupid things that I don't mean in the first place. I told Vanessa I was sorry. I don't think she forgave me, but I hope you will.

Love, Amanda A

191

The problem was, I didn't want to have to see Mrs. Gandy until after she'd had a chance to read my note.

I got a hall pass for the bathroom during math, and I walked as fast as I could down the stairs to the basement.

The door to Sporty's office was partly open. I could hear Sporty singing, almost like he was talking to himself.

Gonna float on my back in the water
And look straight up into the sky,
And feel that cool stream calm my fever
As it whispers a sweet lullaby.
I'll forget that I ever had burdens,
Or troubles, or worries, or fears,
Gonna float on my back in the water
For, oh, about five hundred years.

It sounded like a hymn. I knocked on the door. Sporty said, "Oh, now then, what brings you to see me this afternoon?"

He was sitting in a wooden chair, tipped back on two legs. Teachers hated it when *we* sat like that. I handed him my note, folded twice with "Mrs. Gandy" written on the outside. Sporty took it and looked at the front of it, then at the back. "What's this now?"

"It's a note to Mrs. Gandy," I said. "Will you see that she gets it? Please?"

Sporty brought his chair down on all four legs. "I gotta be the janitor, the guidance counselor, and the baby-sitter,

192

might as well be the postman, too. I'll take care of it for you."

But I worried that Sporty would forget to give Mrs. Gandy the note, and then I worried that he would remember. Then I worried that I'd said it all wrong.

I worried the rest of the afternoon. I had never been so nervous in my life.

I waited until I knew Vanessa would be gone before I walked downstairs. I walked down the long, shadowy hallway on the sides of my feet, so that my outside anklebones were almost touching the floor. My briefcase felt heavier when I walked like that.

I hadn't gotten very far when Mrs. Gandy came out of her classroom. I guess she had been standing in the doorway, looking for me. She came toward me with her arms outstretched.

"Come here to me, my lamb," she said. "Don't you know you don't ever have to be afraid of Mrs. Gandy?"

CHAPTER 30

"I know you're a good girl, with a good heart," Mrs. Gandy said. "And it's like you told me yourself in that note you sent me, you've still got things to learn, and plenty of time to learn them. Well, now you've learned that you can't go around spouting out the same trash that you've heard other people say, without it hurting somebody. Words can hurt people, just like fists can hurt them. Not only that, but I expect you learned that you hurt *yourself,* too, when you use ugly words."

I nodded, looking down at the keyboard. I had learned that.

"Okay, now we're going to start out fresh, me and you. How does that sound?"

It sounded too good to be true. "That would be great." I put my music book, turned to "Jesu, Joy of Man's Desiring," on the music rack, and ran my hand down the middle so it would stay open. My hand shook until Mrs. Gandy reached over and took it in hers. I squeezed her hand so hard that a tear fell out of my eye and landed on my lap.

"All right, then," Mrs. Gandy said. She gave my hand a little shake, then let it go. "And speaking of starting out fresh, don't you think it's time to move on to another piece, other than 'Jesu'?"

I took a deep breath to make sure I wasn't going to cry. "It might be time," I said, "but I wanted to tell you something. I know we talked about 'Silver Bells' and 'O Holy Night,' but I think I'd like to play 'Jesu' as my piece in the school Christmas program. I know it's not a Christmas song, but it's about Jesus, so I thought it might be all right."

Mrs. Gandy thought about that. "I think you have something there," she said. "It may not be a *traditional* Christmas song, but, honey, by the time you're through, it will be."

As a surprise, Mrs. Gandy had brought in an album of music by Bach, and she played the "Little Fugue" for me— or as the album cover said, "Fugue in G Minor (the 'Little')." I was always trying to pretend that life was like music. I wanted it to tick along as happy as "My Grandfather's Clock." But life was more like complicated music, like the "Little Fugue." In the beginning, it sounded like fairies running around on lily pads, trying to learn to fly. Then some of them started flying, and they flew faster and higher—until the music changed. Suddenly the giant from "Jack and the Beanstalk" barged in, stamping on the ground and shaking the lily pads so that the fairies fell off and got wet. I had forgotten about that part of the music. But once the giant had stomped through, he disappeared around the bend, and the fairies could fly again.

My grandma Braverman came to spend Thanksgiving weekend with us, and begged me to play "Jesu, Joy of Man's

Desiring" for her. So finally I went into the living room and sat down at the piano, and Mom and Grandma came in and sat down together on the couch. I pulled out my music book and turned to the right page.

"I don't know what's come over Amanda," I heard Mom say. She didn't think I could hear her. "You ought to hear the way she plays the piano now. She used to be so proper, careful to hit every key, trying to make everything perfect. Now she just rolls with it, and she might hit a sour note every once in a while, but she sure is a lot more fun to listen to."

Of course, Grandma thought I sounded like one of the angels in Heaven, but *she* never did see anything wrong with my playing, like Mom apparently did.

It was right about then, I guess, that the pressure started to get to me, and I kind of snapped. I practiced "Jesu, Joy of Man's Desiring" so much that Dad moved the television into the basement so he could hear the news. I was driving my whole family crazy.

Laura started going to the library to study. "I love your piano playing, Little Bit," she told me, "but *mon Dieu!*"

Mom said, "Amanda, you are really overdoing this, you know."

"I can't help it," I said. "It just feels like, the music is so *perfect,* that if I can play it perfect, then it's like the magic spell has been completed, and everything will *be* perfect."

"The only way to play it perfectly is to enjoy playing it," Mrs. Gandy told me. "You are not going to be able to bang this piece out like it's killing you and have everybody clap.

No. You must play it for yourself, like nobody else is even in that room, and you must play it with your whole heart. You know how you played 'Grandfather's Clock'?"

"That's a baby song," I said. I felt like throwing my music book across the room.

"Well, I disagree with you," Mrs. Gandy said. "I certainly do. You played that song like you were having some fun. That's how you must learn to play this one. Now relax these tight shoulders!" She put her big hands on my shoulders and began to knead them like bread dough. "Loosen up!"

When my lesson was over, I left the music room and walked really fast down the shadowy hallway, still hearing the music in my head the way it was *supposed* to sound. The way Mrs. Gandy played it when she showed me how to improve my technique. *She* could make it sound like waves of water rolling onto a beautiful beach. I got halfway down the hall when Sporty came out of the janitor's closet with a mop and bucket.

"Hey, there, Sporty," he said. "Better tighten up, there."

I stopped walking. "Sporty," I said. "You tell me to tighten up, but Mrs. Gandy just got through telling me I had to loosen up. Now, what am I supposed to do?"

Sporty put the bucket down on the floor and leaned against his mop handle. "Well, now, I tell you the truth. You better be listenin' to Mrs. Gandy, is what I think." He picked up the bucket and started down the hall toward Mrs. Gandy's room. "Yes, sir, I'd do just exactly what that lady say," he said as he walked away.

"Yeah, that's what I thought, too," I said.

By now most days were too cold or rainy to play outside, so we played in the gym a lot. We learned a new game that Gaylyn called Chinese jump rope. Two girls sat on the floor across from each other. They held the ends of two long bamboo sticks, one in each hand. Keeping the sticks about six inches apart, they started a rhythm. They tapped the sticks twice against the gym floor, then brought them up about four inches off the ground and tapped them together twice. One girl hopped in and out while the sticks were moving, trying to keep from getting her feet caught between the sticks. It was neat.

The black girls had played before, but none of us white girls had ever done it. Amy and I caught on pretty quick, but Carolyn Lohmann never could get her foot in the right place at the right time. "My ankles are sore!" she yelled after about the fifth time she'd gotten one caught between the sticks. She finally gave up and joined the girls who were jumping rope. Other girls were sitting on the bleachers, waiting their turns. Victoria tried to braid Robin's stick-straight, light brown hair while they waited.

"Girl, your hair is so soft and fine," Victoria said. "I can't get it to hold a braid." As she made each one, she took a little plastic butterfly clip off of one of her own braids and used it to hold Robin's in place. Victoria's hair stayed braided without the clips. Because of the alphabet, in our classroom Robin sat with Victoria on her left and another black girl, Beatrice Young, on her right. Robin was one of those little girls who was always a foot shorter than anybody else in the class. Victoria and Beatrice had sort of adopted Robin, and they treated her like she was a baby sister, or like a mascot.

"Amanda, your turn!" Darlene called, and I jumped off the bleachers and took my place in front of Gaylyn and Darlene, who were working the bamboo sticks. I liked the sticks better than the rope because of the noise they made as they tapped against the wooden gym floor. It was exciting trying not to get caught. Now that they knew I could do it, Gaylyn and Darlene started moving the sticks faster and faster, trying to trip me up. We were all laughing, and then of course I got caught. I hopped away from the sticks on one foot, dragging the "caught" foot behind me like it had been crushed.

Henry saw me hopping. He left the boys, who were running relay races on the other side of the gym.

"Don't be messing up my girl's jumping feet!" Henry said.

"Come on, Henry," Gaylyn said. "You such a tough man. Come on and see can we catch your big old feet."

Henry jumped right between the sticks, and as Gaylyn and Darlene started tapping them, he made a face like he was a rich, sophisticated woman with his nose in the air and his mouth pulled down, and he hopped once or twice. "Oh, dear me," he said in a high voice, "my big old girdle is slipping down to my knocky-knees."

I sat down on the bleachers because I was laughing too hard to stand up.

The other boys came over to watch and cheer Henry on.

When Gaylyn and Darlene finally caught his foot between the sticks, he acted like he'd been hit by a train or something and fell to the floor in a big pile.

Henry sat up. "Now that is a sight," he said. He pointed up to the bleachers at Robin. She was trying to look at her new braids in Victoria's purse mirror.

The next Saturday morning I went out in the woods to look for two long, straight branches to use for Chinese jump rope. I wandered around awhile, but I knew that I wouldn't be able to play unless I got Mom and Dad or Laura to work the sticks for me. So I gave up and went to the Secret Garden. I stood there holding the one good branch I'd found, trying to get the feeling that there were high walls around me, but I couldn't make the walls come this time. My imagination was probably drying up.

"Amanda!"

I went around the corner of the house. Mom was hanging out the back door. "Want to go shopping with me? I'm going to Thruway Center."

"Okay," I said. I'd been begging her to take me to get some Christmas presents. I threw my stick down and ran to the house to grab my purse.

The Thruway Shopping Center had a grocery store, a drugstore, Amy's Hallmark, a bookstore, Sears, and an underground part. All the best stuff was underground—a branch of the public library, a cheese shop that gave out free samples, and a little art gallery. Best of all was the Curiosity Shoppe.

The Curiosity Shoppe had incense and candles and silk flowers and painted wooden backscratchers and coasters made of woven straw. For the holidays they had two huge Christmas trees set up, with all kinds of neat ornaments on them. I got a little reindeer ornament for Miss Gohagan, but I didn't see any ornaments that I thought were right for Mrs. Gandy. I circled those trees so many times I'm surprised I didn't wear a hole in the carpet, and some of the other customers were beginning to give me strange looks.

That's when I saw it. Next to a display of candles and candleholders was a Christmas decoration hanging on a hook against the wall. It was made to look like an antique piece of sheet music. It had been unrolled except for a little bit still curled at the top and bottom. The music was "Silent Night." The top part of the roll had a red velvet ribbon running through it to hang it up with, and there was a little cluster of fake holly and stuff glued to the bottom. It was *perfect*. (Well, it would have been even more perfect if the music had been "Jesu, Joy of Man's Desiring," but it was still perfect.) I went to the cash register, and the man who rang it up looked at me kind of funny. My face felt hot, and I was so excited I could hardly stand still.

"Looks like you found just what you wanted," he said as he handed me the bag.

"I *did*!" I said. "I just love this store so much!"

He smiled and reached down underneath the counter and brought up a white gift box and a red satin bow. It was the kind of bow that stores *charge money* for. "Merry Christmas," he said.

CHAPTER 31

The auditorium at EWE was so big that when there were only a few people in it, every noise echoed. It was really noisy the day we practiced our Christmas program.

Mrs. Gandy was onstage, directing the Songbirds, one of three fifth-grade choirs. The three sixth-grade choirs were sitting in the audience.

I was backstage, even though I was supposed to be in the audience, too. But Mrs. Gandy had a long way to go before she got to me, and I preferred to sit at the piano and pretend to play "Jesu." The backstage piano was an old upright with some of the ivory chipped off the keys. The piano bench wobbled. The real, onstage piano wasn't new, but it was a baby grand. I hadn't had a chance to play on it yet.

"You not supposed to be back here."

I looked up, and Vanessa was standing in front of me. She wasn't in the Christmas program, so I had no idea what *she* was doing backstage.

"Neither are you," I said.

I moved over on the piano bench. "Sit down," I said. "Do you want to play?"

Vanessa shook her head.

"If you want, I'll teach you how to play something new."

Vanessa didn't budge. "What?" she asked. She looked so funny and cute with her ponytails sticking out over her little tiny ears. I couldn't believe I'd ever thought she was a Beastle.

"Listen," I said. "I really am sorry about what I said to you. Vanessa, I didn't mean it. There's no excuse for what I did, and I wish I could take it back. Please don't keep hating me."

She stared at me. "My mama says don't waste my time hating nobody."

I kept looking down at the piano keys. Vanessa was a little kid, but she was tough. Lucky for me, I was getting tougher, too. I said, "Well, I'd like to try to make it up to you. You know, next year I'll be in West Windsor Junior High, and the year after that you'll be starting there, too. So I want you to remember that when you have to go across town to the new school, I'll be there waiting for you. I know you won't need me to look after you, really, because you'll be a seventh-grader, but I'm going to wait for you where the buses unload, and I'll show you around. I'll make sure you know where the bathrooms are."

She looked at me in that serious way she had. "You can show me around if you want," she said.

Mrs. Gandy heard us talking and made us go sit in the auditorium. Then we all had a surprise: Mrs. Gandy was part of the Christmas program, too. She was going to play a duet with Sporty. He came walking out onstage with his guitar in one hand and a chair in the other. He sat down and tuned his guitar while Mrs. Gandy hit different notes for him. I wondered if they were going to play a blues song for Christmas, but they played "It Came Upon a Midnight Clear." Everybody who heard them could see the stars shining and believe in peace on Earth, goodwill toward men.

My least favorite song in the whole world is the "William Tell Overture"—the Lone Ranger's theme song. I always hear it playing in my head when I'm late or in a hurry, as if all that galloping music is going to help me go faster. The morning of the school Christmas program, I couldn't get my hair to do right to save my life, and I was afraid I was going to miss my bus. There was a hump of hair in the back that had a mind of its own. I tried wetting my hairbrush under the faucet and slicking it down, but that only helped a little bit. I went to the kitchen to find Mom.

"I can't get up in front of the whole school with this hair," I told her, and Dad started laughing, which made me even madder. Mom took me into the bathroom and dried my hair with a towel; then she brushed it out again and sprayed it with some of her hair spray.

"Now I'm going to teach you one of my deepest, darkest secrets," Mom said, looking at me in the bathroom mirror. "It's what I do when all else fails. Just hang your head over and shake your hair out. Now close your eyes, and keep your head down."

She sprayed a couple more puffs. "All right, straighten up."

When I stood up and looked in the mirror, my hair was fluffed out so you couldn't see the hump. It actually looked like it had *body.* Mom smoothed it down just a little with her hands and sprayed it again. "There, what do you think?"

"Cool," I said. "Can I take the hair spray with me?"

"This big can?" Mom said. "No, I'll take it with me when I come to see the program, and I'll give you a squirt backstage. You know, you really look wonderful."

I turned back and looked in the mirror again. I was wearing my favorite dress in the whole world. I had only worn it once before, to church. It was navy blue and made out of material that Mom called crepe. It had long full white sleeves with wide bands of navy around them. The dress was cut so that it curved in the middle and made me look like I had a shape. It had little white faceted buttons down the front, and Mom had let me wear her floating opal necklace, a tear-shaped crystal pendant full of opal flakes.

"Help me put my coat on?" I said. We had to work the big crepe sleeves of the dress into the sleeves of the coat real carefully so they wouldn't get crushed. I buttoned the coat and looked down at the navy blue flats I was wearing for the occasion. The whole process of getting me ready took so much extra time that I missed my bus, but Dad and I jumped in the car and caught up with it at Gordon Grahame's house.

"Wowee," Gordon said. He had one foot on the bottom step of the bus when he saw me jump out of the car wearing my great coat and my best shoes, with big hair.

"Break a leg, beautiful," Dad said. But thank goodness no one on my bus heard him.

I was the next to the last performer on the program, which meant that I had to stand backstage forever waiting. Finally Mr. Harrison announced my name, and I went onstage and sat down at the piano. I could see Mrs. Gandy standing off-stage across from me. I took a deep breath and imagined myself playing "Jesu, Joy of Man's Desiring" like it had never been played before. Then I tried to make it sound like Mrs. Gandy did, like waves and waves of turquoise water with white tops rolling onto a beach. I worked so hard on seeing those waves on that beach that I didn't even think about my hair.

When I finished, I slowly let the pedal back up so that it wouldn't click, and then the applause started. I looked up and saw Mrs. Gandy clapping. She walked out to the middle of the stage and motioned for me to bow. I stood up and bowed, then turned to Mrs. Gandy again.

"That's the way to play that song," Mrs. Gandy whispered, still clapping. "Take another bow, Amanda. You played the tar out of it that time, sugar. Mr. Bach sat up and took notice of that, I know."

I found my seat in the auditorium at the end of the row. I was sweaty and tired, but I felt pretty good.

"Not bad," Henry Bailey said, thumping me on the shoulder. "I thought you was gonna ride that old piano stool right off the stage, you was going at it so hard."

Joy just looked over Henry's head and smiled at me, nodding.

Then we had to be quiet and listen while Mr. Gordon's class came out and sang "White Christmas."

"*White* Christmas?" Henry Bailey whispered. "Now, what I'm saying is why ain't there any songs about a *black* Christmas?"

After the program, Mom told me she was proud of me. "You want to go home now, with me?" she asked. Mr. Harrison had announced that we could do that if our parents were there to take us.

"No," I told her. "I'll go home on the bus." Most of the classes were having Christmas cookies and juice or cleaning out their desks. It felt like the last day of school, almost, when you're really kind of sad about leaving. Plus, I wasn't tired of hearing everybody tell me how good I was on the piano.

Our class had cookies, too, but our desks were already clean, and Miss Gohagan hadn't planned anything else for the day. "I thought perhaps we could talk about some of our family holiday traditions," she said. "Does anyone have a tradition they'd like to share?"

I felt the breeze on the back of my neck when Henry Bailey jumped to his feet. "I know what we ought to do, Miss G.!" he said. "It's a *nice* day outside. We ought to go outside and try to do that Wall again. I got it all figured out this time, Miss. G., I know I do!"

"Well, Henry, I'm not sure that anyone else is interested in going out to the obstacle course this afternoon," Miss Gohagan said.

"Vote!" Henry said, and he moved to the front of the class and turned and faced everybody. "All those in favor of trying to get over the Wall before the end of 1971, raise your hand!"

It took a while, but Henry looked so funny standing up there, and the expression on his face was so pleading, that pretty soon we all raised our hands. I guess the Christmas spirit was in the air.

"Congratulations, Henry," Miss Gohagan laughed. "I see that your politicking has improved considerably. All right, class, let's get our jackets and try to tackle the Wall."

We all stood up and headed for the coats hanging in the back of the classroom. "Today's the day, Amanda Adams," Henry said. "I hope you ate your breakfast cereal this morning because we are about to *boost*."

I grabbed Henry's arm and stopped him. "Henry," I whispered, "I can't do the boost today."

Henry looked at my nice dress and my white tights and my navy blue flats.

"I know," he said. He grabbed my arm and started pulling me toward the back of the room.

CHAPTER 32

"Hey!" Henry called. "Hey, Carolyn Lohmann. Where you going with that bag?"

"To go change clothes, doofus," Carolyn said.

"Now, here's what I'm saying," Henry said. "Amanda Adams has to borrow these extra clothes, because we got to do a little boosting this afternoon at that Wall."

"But—" I started to say, because I had no desire to wear Carolyn Lohmann's gym clothes, but Henry clamped his hand over my mouth. I didn't even think—I just automatically did what every girl I've ever known does when somebody puts a hand over her mouth. I stuck out my tongue. That gets the person's hand all wet and gross. Henry gave me a disgusted look and took his hand off. Then he wiped it on my good dress.

"Carolyn, you won't need those clothes," Henry said. "All we're doing is going over that Wall. You won't be running or jumping, and you won't have no reason to work up a sweat. But Amanda, now, she can't go over the Wall in that dress. You see what I'm saying?"

Carolyn blew a big breath of air out. "Okay, I'll do it for Amanda, *not* for you, Henry." She handed me her bag.

Henry said, "Now, Carolyn, you go help Amanda Adams get changed, and if y'all don't hurry I'm going to come into that girls' bathroom after you. Now I'm going to tell Miss Gohagan that we'll be right along, as soon as you're changed. Hey, Miss G.!"

"Let's go," Carolyn said. "I don't know why I'm doing anything for him, mean as he is, but there's no way you could go over that Wall in your good dress."

We walked down the hall to the girls' rest room, and before we got there, Henry came running up behind us. "It's all fixed," he said. "We're going to meet them at the Wall. Go on in, go on in. I'm just going to wait right here."

When I was finally ready, Henry tried to make us run to the obstacle course.

Once we caught up with the rest of the class, Henry reviewed his plan in his notebook, and then slammed it shut. "Now," he said. "Miss G., you sit down on that swinging log. I'll take over from here. First, we need us a leader. I volunteer. All in favor of me being leader, raise your hands. Keep 'em up, there. See, Miss G.? They know I don't play."

He put his notebook on the log next to Miss Gohagan. "We've got six minutes from the time that stopwatch starts ticking to get everybody over that Wall. Now, you know what you have to do. All I'm saying is, don't mess this up for me. You know what I'm saying?"

It looked like the whole class was hearing the "William Tell Overture," the way everybody was moving, and Henry kept up a stream of chatter. "That's the way, Little Man, scramble up over that Wall. Yes, and Joenathan, you stay on that platform to help those short ones. Here we go, we got it going now. Beastle, stay there with Joenathan and let me see those long arms working. How you doin' over there, Amanda Adams? Umm-hmm. That's it. Just like a machine, Miss G., it's working just like a machine. I *knew* I had this thing planned right—I *knew* I did."

"Two minutes," Miss Gohagan said.

It was my big moment. "All right, Amanda Adams," Henry said. He laced his fingers together and showed me he was ready. "Show us how you can jump, girl."

I got a running start, put my right foot in Henry's cupped hands, and jumped toward the top of the Wall, where Joenathan and Joy were waiting to help pull me over. It felt *great.*

Henry stepped back and bent over, preparing to blast off and run at the Wall. "All right, now, Joenathan, you ready? Hey, Beastle! Get your Beastley long arms ready to pull me up!"

Joy and Joenathan got back in position. But instead of jumping off the platform I stood in the middle, looking down at Henry over the Wall.

"Stop," I said.

CHAPTER 33

Henry raised up and scowled at me, jamming his fists onto his hips. "Amanda Adams, now you know I don't play."

"Henry," I said, "you know how Miss Gohagan said that the mark of a true team is cooperation and courtesy among all the team members? You remember her saying that, Henry?"

Henry threw up his hands and walked in a tight little circle. "Yeah, I remember that. So? Let's *go*, girl."

"So what's your sister's name?"

Henry shook his head like he couldn't believe what he was hearing.

"You don't finish the course until you say it," I said, meeting Henry's glare. One of my knees quivered until I jerked it up straight. I had to risk being Henry's enemy for life. I had to try to do something right.

Joenathan spoke up. "Yeah, Henry—that's fair. Call your sister by her right name."

He didn't say "Joy." It was almost like Joy was under a spell that only Henry Bailey could break.

Henry looked up at us with his mouth open; then he

turned and looked toward Miss Gohagan. She was sitting on the swinging log, looking at her watch. "One minute," she said.

Henry turned back toward the Wall. "If y'all don't quit playing, it's the whole team dead, buried, and gone. Now help me over this Wall."

He and I stared at each other. I said, "She's a person, too, Henry. So what's her name?"

Joy had her head up, listening, with a funny little smile on her face. Everybody else just stood on the ground behind us, waiting.

Henry yelled, *"Marcella Joy Bailey!* Now, haul me up there, fools." He took a running jump and launched himself up the side of the Wall.

Joenathan and I laughed at Henry's scowling face as we reached over and grabbed his hands to haul him over. By the time he had one foot up on the top of the Wall, he was smiling, too, and it was Joy who grabbed his belt loops and pulled him over just as Miss Gohagan said, "Time." (She swears she didn't, but to this day I think she gave us an extra thirty seconds.)

Henry (on purpose, I think) fell onto me, Joenathan, and Joy, but we were all laughing.

"We're *alive!*" Henry yelled. He got up and did a little dance on the platform before he jumped onto the ground. The rest of the team took up the chant. "We're alive!" And they started to clap their hands and whistle.

"We're alive," Henry said, "and the Wall is *down*!"

He looked up at me and spread out his arms. I still stood

on the platform. Both Joenathan and Joy had jumped down after Henry to celebrate with the rest of the team, but I hadn't.

"Get down here, Amanda Adams!" Henry said. He acted like he wanted me to jump into his arms.

I counted the beats to the music that was playing in my head. Then I threw my arms out and jumped toward Henry, and as I jumped I brought my hands up like the conductor at the outdoor concert. I felt the same magic in my hands that he must have felt, pulling music out of the sky.

Vicki Winslow earned a B.A. from the University of North Carolina at Chapel Hill and an M.F.A. in creative writing from the University of North Carolina at Greensboro. She lives in Louisville, Kentucky. Her short stories have appeared in literary journals; *Follow the Leader* won Delacorte's Fourth Annual Marguerite de Angeli Prize for an outstanding first novel for middle-grade readers.